Storm blinked, her eyes suddenly focusing. Chase was staring straight at her, with an expression of baleful suspicion. Quickly Storm looked away, her gut twisting with alarm.

The Moon-Dog was rising over the treetops, though the sky was not yet dark. *And she is white,* realized Storm. The angry red glow of the previous night had vanished. *Has the Moon-Dog forgiven us?*

Or maybe—just maybe—she's telling me that I'm on the right track. . . .

Maybe I'm close to solving the mystery.

SURVIVORS

THE GATHERING DARKNESS

Survivors: Tales from the Packs

NOVELLAS

Also by ERIN HUNTER

WARRIORS

THE PROPHECIES BEGIN

THE NEW PROPHECY

Book One: Midnight
Book Two: Moonrise
Book Three: Dawn
Book Four: Starlight
Book Five: Twilight
Book Six: Sunset

POWER OF THREE

Book One: The Sight
Book Two: Dark River
Book Three: Outcast
Book Four: Eclipse
Book Five: Long Shadows
Book Six: Sunrise

OMEN OF THE STARS

Book One: The Fourth Apprentice
Book Two: Fading Echoes
Book Three: Night Whispers
Book Four: Sign of the Moon
Book Five: The Forgotten Warrior
Book Six: The Last Hope

DAWN OF THE CLANS

Book One: The Sun Trail
Book Two: Thunder Rising
Book Three: The First Battle
Book Four: The Blazing Star
Book Five: A Forest Divided
Book Six: Path of Stars

A VISION OF SHADOWS

Book One: The Apprentice's Quest
Book Two: Thunder and Shadow
Book Three: Shattered Sky
Book Four: Darkest Night
Book Five: River of Fire

EXPLORE THE
WARRIORS
WORLD

NOVELLAS

Hollyleaf's Story
Mistystar's Omen
Cloudstar's Journey
Tigerclaw's Fury
Leafpool's Wish
Dovewing's Silence
Mapleshade's Vengeance
Goosefeather's Curse
Ravenpaw's Farewell
Spottedleaf's Heart
Pinestar's Choice
Thunderstar's Echo

SEEKERS

Book One: The Quest Begins
Book Two: Great Bear Lake
Book Three: Smoke Mountain
Book Four: The Last Wilderness
Book Five: Fire in the Sky
Book Six: Spirits in the Stars

RETURN TO THE WILD

Book One: Island of Shadows
Book Two: The Melting Sea
Book Three: River of Lost Bears
Book Four: Forest of Wolves
Book Five: The Burning Horizon
Book Six: The Longest Day

MANGA

Toklo's Story
Kallik's Adventure

BRAVELANDS

Book One: Broken Pride
Book Two: Code of Honor

THE GATHERING DARKNESS

SURVIVORS

RED MOON RISING

ERIN
HUNTER

HARPER

An Imprint of HarperCollinsPublishers

Library of Congress Control Number: 2017934809
ISBN 978-0-06-234347-5

Typography based on a design by Hilary Zarycky
18 19 20 21 22   CG/BRR   10 9 8 7 6 5 4 3 2 1
❖
First paperback edition, 2018

Special thanks to Gillian Philip

LIGHTHOUSE

HIGH WATCH

WILD PACK CAM

THE ENDLESS LAKE

LONGPAW TOWN

RIVE

PACK LIST

WILD PACK (IN ORDER OF RANK)

ALPHA:

female swift-dog with short gray fur (also known as Sweet)

BETA:

gold-and-white thick-furred male (also known as Lucky)

HUNTERS:

SNAP—small female with tan-and-white fur

BRUNO—large thick-furred brown male Fight Dog with a hard face

MICKEY—sleek black-and-white male Farm Dog

STORM—brown-and-tan female Fierce Dog

PATROL DOGS:

MOON—black-and-white female Farm Dog

TWITCH—tan male chase-dog with black patches and three legs

DAISY—small white-furred female with a brown tail

BREEZE—small brown female with large ears and short fur

CHASE—small ginger-furred female

BEETLE—black-and-white shaggy-furred male

THORN—black shaggy-furred female

OMEGA:

small female with long white fur (also known as Sunshine)

PUPS:

FLUFF—shaggy brown female

TUMBLE—golden-furred male

NIBBLE—tan female

TINY—pale-eyed golden female

PROLOGUE

Darkness lay thick in the den, with only a faint smudge of moonlight shining through the entrance. Lick tried not to shiver as she blinked rapidly. Although the den-smells were warm and comforting, it couldn't be so very cold and lonely out there in the silver glow of the Moon-Dog . . . could it?

Beside her Grunt was still snoring, and Wiggle was making little squeaky noises, his lip quirking back as if he was dreaming of prey. How could her two litter-brothers sleep? The three of them had something to do—something that couldn't wait!

Lick nudged each of her brothers with her nose, shoving Wiggle harder when he grumbled and resisted.

"Wake up," she whispered. "Come *on*. We have to go!"

Grunt gave a tiny groan of protest, but as he woke properly he blinked hard and stumbled to his paws. Then he nipped

Wiggle on the ear to rouse him.

"Hurry up, Wiggle," he growled. "Lick's right. It's time!"

They were making an awful amount of noise, or so it seemed to Lick, but the adult dogs of their new Pack didn't stir. She could hear snores and sleepy murmurs, and the occasional scrape of claws from a dog on a dream-hunt, and she could just make out furred flanks, rising and falling in the darkness. *We'll make it out of here. We have to!*

There was a strange little ache in Lick's belly as she took a last look at Lucky, Martha, Mickey . . . at all the dogs who had cared for them, who had found them and taken them in after their Mother-Dog went to sleep and didn't wake up. This Pack had been kind to them, and Lick wished she could say a proper good-bye.

But if we wake them up, they'll stop us from leaving.

"Come on, Lick." Grunt's low voice was at her ear. "Don't change your mind now! This Pack thinks we're bad dogs. Well, we're real *Fierce* Dog pups, and we'll be fine without them!"

"I know," sighed Lick softly. "I know, it's just that—"

"They're only kind now because we're little." Grunt shook himself angrily and whispered, "They won't be kind when we're big Fierce Dogs and they're scared of us!"

"Of course. We'll never really belong in this Pack." Lick gave her brother a quick nuzzle. "Let's go. But try to be quiet!"

Wiggle was trembling with fear as the pups crept cautiously up the earth slope to the mouth of the den, but Lick and Grunt goaded their smaller brother on with nudges and gentle nips. When they emerged into the faint moonlight, all three of them froze for a moment. The grass beneath Lick's paw pads was damp with dew, and the night air smelled sharp as her nostrils flared. She had to look strong for Wiggle, and that made Lick feel a little braver herself.

But it's a big world out here. . . .

Slowly, quietly, the pups edged forward, huddling together and staying as low as they could. Wet grass tickled Lick's belly and chin, and she wanted desperately to sneeze. *But I can't.*

Up ahead, a large shadow moved against the tree trunks, and Lick shrank back. Along with her brothers, she held her breath as she watched the Patrol Dog Moon slink along the camp's border, her ears pricked and nostrils scenting the air for trouble.

But Moon wasn't scouting for three small pups within the camp itself. Her shape vanished into the shadows, and Lick breathed a sigh of relief. Quickly the three Fierce Dogs scuttled to the tree line that marked the camp's border, their pawsteps sounding terribly loud to Lick's quivering ears.

If the den had felt dark, the woods beyond the camp somehow seemed even blacker. Small creatures rustled in the grass, making the pups jump, and when a night bird screeched overhead, Wiggle started in terror and almost stumbled. Grunt's head was lifted high, his jaw clenched stiffly, and although Lick reckoned his fearlessness was a bit of an act, she didn't want to look like a coward herself. Wiggle was pressed so tightly against her flank, she was sure she was the only thing keeping his trembling little body upright.

"Where's the rock?" asked Wiggle plaintively, when they'd padded in silence for what felt like forever.

"Not far." But Lick was beginning to doubt herself—and she had a feeling Grunt doubted her too, from the resentful glances he was shooting her. If they could just find that oddly shaped gray lump of stone, the one that looked like a crouching giantfur, she'd know exactly where they were, and they could follow the river upstream. . . . "We've passed Giantfur Rock loads of times with Martha. It can't be much farther to the river."

"If we're going the right way," grumbled Grunt.

"Maybe we passed it already?" suggested Wiggle nervously.

"I don't think so." Lick hesitated, one paw in the air.

Grunt glanced to the left and right, licking his small jaws. "I think you've taken us the wrong way, Lick."

"*You're* the one who said we needed to go downwind of that big tree!" Lick snapped.

"And it was you who said we had to cross the little stream!"

Lick opened her jaws to quarrel some more, but she could hear Grunt's breath rasp as he glared at her. His forelegs shook, and she realized he was just as scared as she was.

"It doesn't matter whose fault it is," she whined miserably, her ears drooping. "We're lost and we're all by ourselves and I don't know what we're going to *do*!"

Wiggle gave a despairing whimper and lay down with his head on his paws. "We're lost!" he echoed.

"We'll be all right." Lick tried to comfort him, but she didn't sound convincing even to herself. *We can't be lost. This is silly!* She lifted her head determinedly and sniffed the air. "That way, I'm sure . . . maybe . . ."

The other two just stared, looking very reluctant to believe her.

"Come on!" Forcing her ears up, Lick chose a likely-looking direction and picked up a paw. But it felt heavy, and she realized her legs were aching. Miserably she set down her paw once more, and her ears drooped. "I don't know," she mumbled. "I don't know the way."

Silence fell around the three pups, and they stared at one another in lonely misery and terror. Even the trees' shadows seemed to draw tighter around them.

Then, in the stillness, there was a rattle and rustle of leaves.

Lick couldn't help giving a yelp of shock, and she spun around to face the pale shape that was pushing through the undergrowth toward them. Out of the scrub came a small black nose, quivering whiskers, and then, abruptly, a bright and friendly white-furred face.

"Daisy!" squeaked Lick. The sickening fear gave way to almost unbearable relief, and her small legs suddenly felt weak and shaky.

"Lick! Grunt, Wiggle—what are you doing out here in the middle of the night?" The little white dog gazed at the pups, her dark eyes full of concern. "You could have been hurt!"

Lick and Grunt traded guilty glances, while Wiggle sniffled unhappily, staring at his paws.

"We were running away," blurted Lick at last.

"You were?" Daisy's eyes widened in disbelief. "But why?"

"No dog wants us in this Pack." Grunt's face grew surly and resentful. "We're better off on our own."

"Oh, Sky-Dogs, of course that's not true—not either part!" Daisy sprang forward on her short legs and began to lick them all frantically. "Of *course* we want you in the Pack, pups—and of course you're better off with us! Every dog needs a strong Pack, now that the Big Growl has changed the world!"

"But the Pack Dogs don't like us," muttered Grunt.

"Now, come on back to the camp with me." Ignoring his sullen words, Daisy licked Grunt's nose until he sneezed. "Lucky wants you in our Pack, and so does Mickey. And Martha, and me. And if any dog doesn't, they'll soon come around. Don't you worry, pups!"

Lick exchanged a look with Grunt. Wiggle was clearly desperate to go back with Daisy; his eyes were suddenly brighter and his pricked ears quivered with frantic hope. Grunt looked too tired to argue anymore. And if Lick was honest, she felt very relieved indeed that they'd been found.

"All right, Daisy." She couldn't stop a yawn from escaping, and her jaws widened with it till her eyes were squeezed tight. She shook herself and blinked rapidly. "We'll come. But it's such a long way back. . . ."

"Oh, little one." Daisy laughed fondly. "It's not half as far as you think. You've barely reached the edge of the first hunting ground."

Lick's ears drooped and her body sagged. *So much for our big escape. And no wonder we couldn't find Giantfur Rock. It's still far, far away.*

All the same, she felt her heart lighten a little as she followed in Daisy's pawsteps. Exhausted as she was, she only wanted to curl up in that cozy den once again, and not even Grunt's rebellious muttering behind her could change her mind.

And I do want to belong to this Pack. Maybe Daisy's right. They'll get used to us, and they'll like us in the end.

I want my Mother-Dog, but she's gone to sleep forever.

So I want to belong. I want a Pack.

Lick glanced skyward with a terrible pang of yearning. *Why can't I belong?*

CHAPTER ONE

Drowsy and content, Storm lay stretched out in the Sun-Dog's light. The peace of the glade was broken only by the squeaks and yelps of the four pups who romped and played outside their den, as their parent-dogs, Alpha and Lucky, looked on. One eye open, one ear pricked, Storm watched them. There was a strange warm feeling in her chest. For some reason, she realized with surprise, just watching the pups' playtime made her happy.

The little dogs were so joyful and carefree, as if the terror of their near drowning in the Endless Lake had been completely forgotten. Storm was glad the experience hadn't affected them too badly, and she could understand why: Lucky, the Pack's Beta, had a way of making the tiniest of pups feel secure and cared-for . . .

. . . *even a pup who isn't his own.* Storm felt a twinge of gratitude as memories of her own turbulent puphood came back to her. She and her brothers had had nowhere else to go, no dog to take care of them, but Lucky had stepped in to take the place of their parent-dogs. Despite Lucky's love and care, she thought with a pang of loss, her brothers hadn't made it in the end. . . .

But I did. I survived, and now I live for all three of us. And that's because of Lucky.

The atmosphere of peace in the camp felt reassuring. It was good to see her Packmates, young and old, looking so content. The whole camp felt bathed in happiness and goodwill. The Pack needed a break from the suspicion and fear that had haunted them for so long. This sun-high it seemed every dog had decided to push the problem to the back of their minds. Many of them believed that the traitor in their ranks—the bad dog who had done so many terrible things—had been Arrow, her fellow Fierce Dog, who had left the Pack with Bella. They thought that with Arrow gone, they must be safe.

It was so tempting to believe that . . . but Storm was *sure* that Arrow was innocent. And if that was true, then the bad dog who had laced the prey pile with clear-stone and framed the loyal Patrol Dog Moon for stealing prey had not been found. Whisper's murder had still not been solved.

Storm suppressed a shiver at the memory of Whisper's death.

The threat was still real—she knew it, even if she wished she didn't. The bad dog could right now be planning another attack. But even so, in this moment she couldn't help enjoying the new peaceful spirit among her Packmates.

I just wish I could believe it was over. . . .

Storm raised her head from the ground and caught sight of Snap. The hunt-dog was padding toward her, her jaws full of soft moss. Her ears were pricked, her tail wagging.

Snap set the moss gently down beside her. "Storm! I brought this for you—I thought you looked a little uncomfortable. Here, put it under your forepaws."

Storm blinked, grateful and surprised. She hadn't really noticed before, but her forepaws were resting awkwardly on hard stone. Half rising, she pawed the moss onto the flat boulder beside her and sank down again. Now her stretched-out paws felt as if they were floating on air. "Thank you, Snap, that was thoughtful."

And unexpectedly kind, she thought as she watched Snap nod and pad away. Mickey's mate could be short-tempered—and what was more, Snap had been one of the dogs who suspected that the traitor must be a Fierce Dog. With Arrow gone, those dogs' suspicions had fallen squarely on Storm herself. Now, though, Snap seemed to regard Storm as a hero. Every dog here knew that it was she—the Fierce Dog—who had dived into the Endless Lake and pulled Tiny out, saving the little pup's life with a trick Martha had taught her long ago.

It's a really nice change, thought Storm. *I'm not sure I realized just how much their suspicion was upsetting me until they started trusting me again.*

Sighing contentedly, she let her eyes drift shut. Spots of light danced behind her eyelids, and she observed them dreamily till they dissolved into blackness. That was when the less pleasant thoughts began to drift in: *But I know we can't afford this sense of peace. After all that the traitor dog has done . . . spreading blood and panic in the camp, killing that fox cub to cause a war between dogs and foxes . . .*

She wished she could believe those terrible crimes had been committed by one of the dogs who had already left the Pack. It couldn't have been Bella or Arrow, of course—Storm knew they weren't capable of such evil, however much the other dogs distrusted them.

But what about the dogs of Terror's old Pack? What about Ruff, or Woody, or Rake? Or even Dart, who had been in the Wild Pack from the beginning but had left it to join up with those three deserters? They'd been gone by the time the rabbit blood was smeared all over the glade, true, but they could have sneaked back somehow to plant it. . . .

Another warm flank settled down against hers, and she opened her eyes to see that Mickey and Snap had joined her in her patch of sunlight. Instantly she felt reassured again. Storm felt small paws on her back and turned her head as Lucky and Alpha's pups began to clamber all over her, swatting her tail and nibbling at her ears. "Tiny!" she yelped at the smallest of them.

Tiny took no notice, chewing happily on one ear as the bigger, shaggier Tumble rolled off and began to attack Storm's hindpaw. The two other female pups, Nibble and Fluff, seemed to be fighting to the death along Storm's spine, and when she shook them off, they climbed straight back on and charged at each other again.

"I'd give in, if I were you." Mickey laughed beside her.

Storm rolled onto her side and batted idly at Tiny, who yelped in delight. Nibble and Fluff, forgetting their tussle, threw themselves at Storm's throat and chewed it with their small soft mouths, growling and giggling. Storm gave a dramatic groan of defeat and waved her paws in the air. Tumble jumped onto her shoulder and began to yap, tossing his small head in triumph.

"Pups, pups, I'm beaten!"

"Grrrrr!" Tiny had most of one of Storm's paws in her jaws.

"We've conkw . . . conqu-wered the Fierce Dog!" cried Tumble.

"Hooray!" barked Fluff and Nibble.

Storm lay helplessly beneath them, grunting out laughs. Deep in her belly she could feel that unaccustomed warmth and affection. *They're not even a little bit afraid of me anymore. Not since I rescued them from the Endless Lake. In fact, I think they really like me. . . .*

"Storm, Storm! Tell us a story!" Nibble was prancing up and down right in front of her nose.

"Yes, a story!" chorused Fluff and Tiny.

"Or we'll beat you again!" growled Tumble, right in Storm's ear, making her jump.

"Oh, I'd love to, pups. . . ." Storm half rose, shaking herself. *Especially since you've all finally learned to say "Storm" instead of "Torm"!* "But—hold on, Tumble, don't bite me!—I can't think of one . . . wait . . ."

"*I'll* tell you a story." Alpha's amused voice came from behind them. "So long as you leave Storm alone, pups. Let's give her some peace!" The beautiful swift-dog licked Storm's muzzle affectionately, and then settled down on the grass. The pups finally abandoned Storm and nestled eagerly against their Mother-Dog—all except Tiny, who stayed firmly between Storm's paws. Storm gave her a gentle lick on the top of her head.

Alpha winked solemnly at Storm, and Storm thumped her

tail gratefully. "I'll tell you another story of the Wind-Dogs if you like, pups."

"Oh, the Wind-Dogs!" Fluff barked excitedly, her shaggy dark-brown ears shooting up. All the pups loved Alpha's stories of her favorite Spirit Dogs. Alpha, like all swift-dogs, was closely connected to the Wind-Dogs. That gave the pups a special relationship with them, too.

"Well," began Alpha, crossing her forepaws and settling down to tell her tale. "You all know that with every turn of the four seasons, the Wind-Dogs chase the Golden Deer around the world. And that every year, when the Golden Deer is caught, Long Light dies, and Red Leaf begins as the Earth-Dog prepares for Ice Wind."

"Yes, yes, yes. We remember." Excitedly Tumble climbed over Nibble to hear better, and she shook him off.

"In the proper order of things, the Golden Deer rises again with Tree Flower and the start of the next Long Light. But once, many years ago, Long Light passed without the Wind-Dogs catching the Golden Deer."

Fluff gasped. "How did that happen?"

"No dog knows, pups. But because the Golden Deer ran free,

Red Leaf never came, and neither did Ice Wind. The Wind-Dogs chased the Deer anyway, pursuing it fiercely, desperately, but they were tired—*so* tired—and they were afraid that this time, it would never be caught. But if the Deer ran free forever, it would put the whole world out of balance!"

The four pups could only stare at their Mother-Dog, wide-eyed. Storm watched them with amusement.

"Finally the Wind-Dogs ran out of breath and it seemed as though the Deer would run forever. What was to become of the land without Red Leaf and Ice Wind? Without the cold seasons, plants and trees cannot rest and grow!

"But that, pups, was when the first Swift-Dog arose from her den. She was shocked to see the Golden Deer still running free. But she knew what to do." Alpha's face grew solemn. "She sprang to her paws and ran alongside the Wind-Dogs—she could catch up with them, because unlike them, she was fresh and rested. 'Look,' she said, 'how my body is light, and my legs so long and thin. I can run, and I'm not tired. Let me carry on the chase!'

"Well, the Wind-Dogs were so tired by now that they agreed to let the first Swift-Dog take her chance. And soon they saw that she was right: Her body was as light and agile as a bird in flight, and her long legs ate up the ground. The Golden Deer had run far and fast, pups—but it too was tired now. Up a long hill it raced, with the brave Swift-Dog gaining on it. And when the two reached the summit, the Swift-Dog gave a mighty leap—*and brought down the Golden Deer!*"

The pups were beside themselves with excitement, yapping and squeaking. "Yay! The first Swift-Dog!"

"And so balance was restored to the world. The Wind-Dogs were pleased with the first Swift-Dog, proud of her bravery and determination. So they swore that from that moment on, any mortal dog who caught the Golden Deer—or one of its shadows— would be granted long life and good luck, for them and their pups and their Pack."

"Hooray!" barked Tumble, spinning around in delight. "One day I'll catch it!"

"No, *I* will!" yapped Fluff, shoving him with a paw.

"Me! Me!" squeaked Tiny, making all of them laugh.

Storm managed not to join in the laughter, however affection- ate. She gave the little pup a gentle nuzzle. *I wouldn't risk hurting her feelings.* "Why shouldn't you catch the Golden Deer, Tiny? You're very brave and determined."

Tiny gazed up at her with adoration. "Thank you, Storm!"

There were some dogs in the Pack who thought the Golden

Deer was nothing more than a story, a fable to tell pups. *But I know differently*, thought Storm, excitement and anticipation stirring in her belly. *I've seen it. Lucky almost caught it, not so long ago. He got within leaping distance of its shadow. . . .*

Storm watched the pups as they began to yawn and settle. *If life in the Pack stays quiet, I could go out hunting for it before the end of Long Light. Not just for Tumble, Nibble, Fluff, and Tiny; I could do it for the Pack, too . . . prove how grateful I am that they've accepted me. And it would show them, finally, that this is where I belong.*

Abruptly filled with energy, Storm jumped to her paws. "Alpha, is it all right if I go for a run now—on my own? That story made me want to stretch my legs!"

Alpha looked a little taken aback, but she nodded. "Of course, Storm. And I know what you mean. Talking about running makes me want to run, too!" She glanced at her pups and gave an amused sigh and a shake of her head. "Not right now, though . . ."

With a last nuzzle of Tiny's shoulder, Storm turned and bounded out of the camp. *I probably won't see the Golden Deer, but who knows? Perhaps it's still around. At least it's worth a try! If I can just catch the scent—*

But it wasn't the scent of deer that filled her nostrils as she raced through the underbrush. It was the smell of a familiar dog, and she was almost on top of him before she skidded to a halt.

"Bruno!"

Storm's heart sank a little. Bruno had never quite accepted her as a member of the Pack, and he had a deep mistrust of all Fierce Dogs. Even during these last few days when the rest of the Pack had been so nice to Storm, Bruno had still been standoffish. She hadn't expected to run into the big dog, but he was on patrol, of course. The Pack's numbers had dwindled so badly, even hunt-dogs were having to take their turn on patrol duty. Storm stiffened and tucked her ears back, waiting for a snide comment.

"Storm." Bruno too looked somewhat surprised, but his brown eyes softened as he watched her. "You're out patrolling too?"

"Just a run," she muttered. "I'd better get going—"

"Storm, wait." Bruno took a pace toward her. "Just a moment. I need to say something. I'm—I'm sorry . . . for how I've behaved."

Storm felt her jaw hang loose. She could only stare at Bruno in distrust.

"I mean it," he went on. "I've been unfair to you, and I apologize. I don't think you're the bad dog, I really don't."

Storm sat back and scratched her ear with a hindpaw, playing for time. *Am I hearing this right?* "But you don't like Fierce Dogs—"

"I still think Arrow must have killed Whisper," Bruno

mumbled. "Well, it was either him or one of the foxes. But I watched you save Tiny from the Endless Lake, and I knew that I'd been wrong about you. You're a good dog, Storm. I'm sorry I didn't believe you. And I'm sorry for all the trouble I've caused you."

Storm stared at his mournful, penitent face. How many times had she seen it twisted with meanness and suspicion? However carefully she examined it now, she just couldn't make out if there was something harder behind his remorseful eyes. *How can I trust him?*

She stood up again on all four paws. "But you're still blaming Arrow. You still think all Fierce Dogs are bad. We didn't *ask* to be born Fierce Dogs."

"Arrow's different." His eyes were beseeching. "I *do* still suspect him. We don't know him, not really, we never did. And now he's left the Pack, and taken Bella with him. But it's not about him being a Fierce Dog, Storm. I won't ever judge you for that again. I know now it was stupid."

Storm licked her chops. Bruno did look genuinely upset. Could she really keep arguing with that miserable expression? "If that's true, Bruno, then . . . I guess I can accept your apology."

"It is true, I promise. Listen, Storm, I have to go catch up with my patrol." The big dog's ears were pricked eagerly, but all of a sudden he crouched, his paws stretched out, his head lowered close to the ground. "But please believe me when I say I regret all of it."

He wouldn't fake that submission, would he? He's always said exactly what he thought. Storm pinned her ears back, shocked but reluctantly pleased. *I would never have expected Bruno to care about my feelings. But hard as it is to believe, I think he's for real.* Tentatively she began to wag her tail.

"All right. . . . All right, Bruno. And thanks. I . . . appreciate you saying this."

"Good." Bruno darted forward to touch her nose with his. "Thanks, Storm. That means a lot to me."

As she watched his retreating haunches, Storm sat back again, flummoxed but filled with growing happiness. *I can hardly believe it. Bruno meant that, I'm sure of it. He doesn't hate me anymore. The whole Pack accepts me.*

Things really are getting better. This is where I belong.

CHAPTER TWO

The grave was such a peaceful place. Shaded by trees, surrounded by the scents of the forest, dappled in sunlight. Storm stood by it, gazing down at the place where the Pack had brought Whisper to return to the Earth-Dog. The ground no longer looked freshly turned; mosses and grass and tiny purple flowers grew on its surface. Whisper was becoming part of the land again, part of the forest, just as the Earth-Dog promised all dogs.

It felt right. Storm bowed her head, then turned to leave.

And jumped, her heart thrashing. Whisper himself stood before her: not part of the earth after all, but himself again, his eyes bright but fearful, his ears pinned back.

"Don't forget me, Storm, all right?"

Her throat felt dry, but Storm shook her head. She rasped, "Of course I won't forget you, Whisper! But we need to move on . . . the whole Pack needs to look to the future."

Sadness filled the gray dog's eyes, and he shook his head. "Oh, Storm."

Storm's belly felt cold, and she shuddered. She couldn't take her eyes off Whisper's.

"You can't move forward yet, Storm. Please." He gestured with his head. "First you have to look behind you."

She didn't want to turn and look, but she had no choice. Fur prickling, she turned, slowly.

Two graves.

Two graves.

Whisper's grave was just as it had been, settling into the life of the forest, the undergrowth beginning to creep across his resting place.

But beside his, a second grave was freshly dug, the turned earth dark and moist.

"Who?" Storm barked, her voice choked and harsh. "Whose is it, Whisper?"

She heard only silence. When she glanced back, Whisper had vanished. Frantically Storm began to dig, clawing at the earth, kicking it clear with her hind legs. She dug and dug, desperate. The soil was loose, and easy to pull up, and she was soon deep down in the grave, deeper than they'd ever buried Whisper. Still she clawed and kicked, and still there was no body, no dog.

Where is the corpse? How far down must I dig? Storm jerked up her head and howled aloud into the shadowy forest.

"Whose grave is this? Whose?!"

* * *

She started awake in her own den, shaking violently. Terrified, she peered at her paws. She was relieved to see there was no mud on her claws—she had not been digging in her sleep.

But it felt as if she had. She could imagine the dirt's grittiness caught between her paw pads; she could even taste it in her mouth. And as much as she spat and shook herself, she couldn't get rid of it.

It was early; the Sun-Dog had not yet shown his shining hide through the trees, though the promise of his glow had paled the edge of the sky. Storm shuddered, trying not to whine. *I didn't wake any other dog, thrashing around. Oh, thank the Sky-Dogs. How could I ever have explained this horrible dream?*

The taste of dream-mud, and the sensation of dirt in her claws, stayed with her all morning; she could not forget the sight of that fresh grave next to Whisper's. *I never found a body. But Whisper was trying to tell me something, I know it.*

Will another dog die? Who will it be?

Me?

She still hadn't managed to shake off the fear by the time she joined Beetle and Thorn for their early patrol. The two dogs greeted her with friendly enthusiasm, but Storm herself struggled to look cheerful. She was irrationally certain that her fur was filthy with grave dirt.

"What's wrong, Storm?" Beetle furrowed his brow.

She shook herself for the umpteenth time, though there was nothing to dislodge. *It was a dream, for the Sky-Dogs' sake.* "Nothing. Let's go."

The two litter-siblings exchanged doubtful glances, but Storm gave them no time to ask more questions. She led them on their familiar route, heading in a wide circle toward the longpaw town. There had been more activity in the deserted settlement lately, and Alpha wanted every dog to keep a close eye on the goings-on.

The three dogs slowed their pace as a shattered line of low buildings came into view. With a nod to Thorn and Beetle, Storm lowered her shoulders and crept through the long grass, her ears quivering with alertness. A sharp scent came to her nostrils: tangy and piney, like a freshly broken branch.

Alpha's right. The longpaws are back. And they've been busy.

There were fences now, their wood white-pale, smelling freshly cut by sharp longpaw weapons. The ground had been flattened out in long, dark strips. Beside the strips of flattened soil, great square holes had been excavated, and more fresh-cut wooden posts had been driven into their edges. Slumbering nearby were the vast yellow loudcages the longpaws used to dig and flatten and smash.

"Don't wake the loudcages," whispered Beetle, his tail stiff and quivering.

"I don't think we will," murmured Storm. "They've obviously been hard at work."

Thorn's eyes were narrowed, and her hackles were raised. Both the litter-siblings looked nervous and hostile; they hated longpaws, and no wonder—their Father-Dog, Fiery, had been captured and killed by particularly vicious ones. Again Storm recalled that terrible evening when Lucky and Alpha's pups had splashed recklessly into the Endless Lake and almost drowned. Thorn was one of the dogs who had gone to save the pups, but just when it had mattered most, she couldn't bring herself to set a paw on the beach—because there had been longpaws there. Her fear had defeated her, brave as she was.

"Are you two all right?" Storm growled, glancing at both dogs with concern.

"We're fine." Thorn's voice sounded choked, but there was a determined light in her eyes. "Let's keep going."

"Stay close together, then," Storm said. "We'll be safe if we protect each other."

Even more cautiously than before, they slunk through the grass toward the town. Storm could sense the fear and anger emanating from Thorn and Beetle; their fur was rank with it, but they pressed on bravely. Tall, shadowy figures moved in the half-destroyed buildings, and the three dogs could hear the barks of longpaws communicating with one another.

"I can't stand the thought of longpaws so close to our camp," whispered Thorn. "After what they did to our Father-Dog."

Beetle shuddered. "Longpaws are bad, Storm."

"These might be different longpaws," suggested Storm uncertainly. "The better kind, like the one on the beach that Mickey rescued from the giant wave. These ones don't have the shiny black face masks that hide their eyes, or the yellow fur."

I'm trying to convince Beetle and Thorn, but I'm not even convincing myself. They're probably right. And this can't be good for the Pack. Even that nice longpaw on the beach tried to make Mickey go with him in the loudbird. . . .

Worse, the deep pits and the ravaged earth of the settlement reminded her of the grave from her dream. Storm's fur prickled and her hackles quivered. *It's all wrong. Something terrible is coming: The dream told me so, and all this longpaw activity only makes it more certain.*

But I can't put my paw on what it will be. . . .

* * *

27

"To me, Pack, and listen for a moment."

Alpha was sitting up, watching the Pack patiently as the lowest-ranking dogs finished eating their share of the prey pile. The Moon-Dog, only her half-turned haunches visible, was still low on the horizon; but higher in the sky, there were dark clouds, and occasional drops of rain fell on the gathered Pack. Normally they would all hurry to their dens now, but Alpha looked serious and intent, and her dark eyes glowed with determination. Every dog sat up and paid attention. Sunshine, the Omega, swallowed her last bite of mouse, licked her paws clean, and pricked her feathery ears.

Alpha nodded in satisfaction. "Now. We need to discuss the longpaws Storm, Beetle, and Thorn saw on their patrol today. There are many more of the longpaws than before, and they and their giant loudcages are making great changes to the land. Will they come closer to the camp? And if they do—how will we respond?"

In the thoughtful silence that followed her statement, two dogs jumped to their paws, growling. Beetle and Thorn, Storm realized with surprise.

"We attack them, of course!" Thorn's bark resounded strongly through the glade.

"We drive them away," agreed her litter-brother, his eyes hard. "Before they can do even more damage to our Pack!"

"It's *our* territory," added Thorn. "Not theirs! They abandoned it."

Storm stared at the two litter-siblings, uneasy. She knew there was more to this than the desire to protect their territory. The change in Thorn since this afternoon was striking, and unsettling; clearly she'd regained some of her courage, but what Thorn and Beetle wanted was no less than revenge for Fiery—and that, Storm knew, could never end well. Not against longpaws with loudcages and deadly loudsticks.

"So what do you say, Alpha?" barked Beetle. "Will we defend our territory?"

Alpha stood up on her flat rock and looked sternly at the two of them.

"No," she said, quietly but clearly. "We will not fight longpaws. That has never worked for any dog. You two may be too young to have learned this, but I know it well—and so does Beta, who was in the Trap House with me." She glanced at her mate, Lucky.

Beetle looked surprised and angry at Alpha's calm refusal, but Thorn pricked one ear forward, as if suddenly less sure. "What's a Trap House?"

Storm shifted her attention from Thorn to Alpha. She wanted to know that, too.

"I'll explain, and then you might be less inclined to tangle with longpaws." Alpha lay down again, her paws in front of her. "Long-paws are not content to let free dogs be free, even when we *don't* bother them. They capture free dogs and hold them prisoner in steel cages. These places are cold, and cramped, with barely room for a dog to stand—there's no chance to roll, or run, or jump." She sighed, a sad, faraway look on her narrow face. "And sometimes they take dogs out of those cages, yes—but those dogs disappear, and they are never seen again."

Storm felt a great shudder run through her hide. Beetle still looked angry, but Thorn's rage seemed tinged with fear once more.

"All right," said Thorn after a moment, bowing her head. "We accept your decision, Alpha."

"Of course you do," Alpha answered gently. "I'm sorry, Thorn and Beetle, but this is the only way."

"Looks like we don't have a choice," grumbled Beetle, but he lay down and ducked his ears submissively.

"There's a chance the longpaws might leave us alone." Mickey the Farm Dog stepped forward, the voice of reason as always. "If we don't trouble them, they might not trouble us."

"That's not what happened to Fiery!" snapped Moon, rising to her paws. Then her body sagged, and she sighed. "Longpaws will always hunt us down—just like they hunted down my mate. I'm not angry now, like Thorn and Beetle are. I'm just sad. And I don't want what happened to Fiery to happen to any other dog." She twitched her tail and looked keenly at Alpha. "Will we have to move camp again?"

"I'm not sure." Alpha looked down at the rock beneath her paws. "If the longpaws want this territory, though, we may have no choice."

Storm gasped. Would it really come to that? She'd been so preoccupied with the threat of the traitor within the Pack, she hadn't thought that such danger could come from outside.

Several of the dogs gave angry, protesting growls.

"This is our home!" yelped Snap.

"We've fought so hard, and worked so hard," added Daisy miserably. "This is our home now."

"And it's perfect," whined Sunshine. "The glade, the pool, the cliffs where we can watch for trouble . . ."

"Where would we go?" asked Breeze. "The other dogs who have left the Pack have surely claimed all the best territory nearby. We'd have to travel very far before we could settle again." She glanced at the four small pups, her face full of worry.

"I don't know." Moon sighed, scraping the earth with a claw. "I'd travel any distance to keep my pups safe—and I'm sure Alpha and Lucky think the same. The pups would manage, if we all helped them."

"My brothers and I traveled with Lucky and Mickey, when we left the Dog-Garden," Storm said quietly, half-afraid to remind the Pack of her Fierce Dog home but determined to reassure Breeze. "We were about the same age then. They have a whole Pack, and their Mother-Dog and Father-Dog. They'll be all right."

"I agree," put in Mickey gently, giving Breeze a lick. "Longpaws may not all be bad, but the pups will be safer if we stay away from them."

Third Dog Twitch nodded. "It's a big decision to make, Alpha. Perhaps we shouldn't be too rash, but we should all think hard about our future."

Lucky, who had been quiet till now, gave a growl. Gently he licked Tumble's small head. "It's the pups who are the future of our Pack, and I don't ever want to see them in longpaw cages."

Alpha gave a sharp, quiet bark. "Very well. The discussion is over for now. There's much for every dog to think about. Talk about it among yourselves. We will come together again soon and decide what to do. I know it's a hard bone to chew, my Pack."

In ones and twos, the dogs drifted away toward their dens. Only a little rain had fallen, but cold drops still spattered on their fur as the clouds blustered above them, and Storm found herself tired, and eager for her dry, peaceful den. She set off in its direction, nodding to Chase and Daisy, who were on patrol duty for the night. But just as she was about to enter the welcoming warmth of her den, two shapes caught her eye at the edge of the forest.

Storm hesitated. It was Beetle and Thorn, and they were deep in a quiet, intense conversation. *It must have been tough for them tonight,* she thought, *being told hard truths about the longpaws.* It had to be difficult for the two young dogs to choke down Alpha's ruling: to accept that they could never have revenge for their Father-Dog.

But the litter-siblings were as close as two dogs could be, and Storm knew they were resilient. She would not interfere; everything would be fine. Thorn might be terribly afraid of longpaws, but Beetle was the best dog to reassure his sister, despite his own fears. The two of them had always helped each other since their Father-Dog's death.

They're hurting, and angry, and afraid, Storm realized, *but they've got each other. And I'd probably say the wrong thing anyway. I'm not very good at comforting.*

She turned away, shaking off her unease, and padded into her den to sleep.

CHAPTER THREE

The Sun-Dog's rays were growing warmer by the day, and dazzling spots of light dappled the little freshwater pool. Storm lounged sleepily by Lucky and his pups. Even Tumble, Fluff, Nibble, and Tiny had run out of energy and had flopped in a pile beside their Father-Dog.

It reminded Storm of when the pups were very small, which didn't seem all that long ago. How had the time passed so quickly? Only recently, curling up and snoozing was all they had ever done; they had barely been able to lift their heads or open their eyes. Now, their parent-dogs spent most of their time and energy trying to round them up, and the four pups were constantly chattering and squealing and bouncing and play-fighting. Lucky looked relieved to see them sitting still for a while.

Even as Storm watched them, though, Tumble stirred,

wriggled away from his litter-siblings, and trotted toward the pond. The others were quick to follow, and Lucky gave a small, half-suppressed groan.

Storm laughed softly. "They don't stay still for long, do they?"

"They certainly don't." But there was adoration in Lucky's eyes as he gazed after his pups.

Tumble hesitated, a tail's-length from the pond's edge, and the others followed his example, hanging back warily. It was long moments before the shaggy golden male pup summoned up the courage to dip his forepaws into the pond. He tilted his head uncertainly and retrieved one of his paws. Beside him, Nibble dipped in the very tip of a forepaw. Tiny shrank back, ears low, tail tucked between her legs.

Fluff stepped past Tumble, a determined look on her face. She managed to step into the water with all four paws, and that encouraged the others. Tumble and Nibble took deep, shaky breaths and joined her at the pond's edge; Nibble sniffed at the sun-dappled surface and sneezed.

"It's all right," she said confidently, and took a pace forward.

The bank must have sloped down sharply at just that point. The little tan pup stumbled and fell into the water with a splash, and her three litter-siblings instantly erupted in panicked barks and yelps.

Tiny gave a miserable, terrified howl. "Help, Lucky, help!"

Springing up, Lucky was at the water's edge in an instant, and leaned down and seized Nibble's scruff. Storm too was on her paws, ready to help, but it was obvious that Nibble was fine now. Lucky set the sodden pup down on the bank, and Nibble shook herself violently. She was trembling.

"Nibble," he scolded her gently, "the water there isn't that deep. You wouldn't have been in trouble if you hadn't panicked. And that goes for you three, too." He nodded sternly at Tumble, Fluff, and Tiny. "You must learn to keep calm."

"I'm not going in, even if it isn't deep," yelped Tiny. "Water can eat you."

"Yes, look how the Endless Lake grabbed Tiny!" yapped Fluff.

"The Endless Lake grabbed Tiny because the Lake-Dog is wide awake and lively, and he likes to pull at a dog when you least expect it. And the Endless Lake is so huge, a pup can disappear in it," explained Lucky patiently. "This pond is sleepy and calm. Truly, pups."

"Well, I'm still not going in it again," said Nibble stubbornly.

She shook more water out of her fur and shuddered.

"All right, pups," sighed Lucky. "I'll take you back to the den."

The pups' ears all pricked up with relief, and Tiny turned and aimed a high-pitched growl back at the surface of the pond, as if it were an enemy she had beaten in a fight.

This is wrong, Storm thought, alarmed at Tiny's anger and at Lucky's resignation. *She shouldn't growl at the River-Dog like that! What if they make an enemy of her for life?*

"Wait, Lucky!" Storm padded to his side. "This is crazy. We can't let the pups be scared of water forever."

"That's true," mused Lucky, "but they're still very young, Storm. Maybe we should give them more time."

The pups nodded their enthusiastic agreement.

"Come on, Lucky." Storm straightened her spine and faced her Beta. "This is important. What if we have to cross a stream to reach a new camp? What if they have to escape a giantfur across water?"

"Yes," said Lucky slowly, "you're right. But what are you suggesting, Storm?"

"Martha taught me and Wiggle and Grunt to swim at the same age your pups are now," said Storm firmly. There was a small twinge in her belly as she remembered the huge, gentle water-dog who had been her foster Mother-Dog. "Martha wouldn't want these pups to be afraid of water! I can teach them to have courage, to not fear the water, exactly as Martha taught me. The pups can grow up to be friends with the River-Dog."

"No, Lucky!" exclaimed Nibble. "Don't let Storm put us back in the water!"

Tiny shrank back behind her braver sister. Tumble put on a fierce face, drawing back his lip in a snarl.

Lucky lifted his head, facing Storm. Then he gave her a tiny nod. He turned to his pups.

"Storm's right," he told them sternly. He bent his head to lick Nibble's long snout. "Do you know what we've all learned, pups, all the dogs who survived the Big Growl?"

They shook their heads, wary and nervous.

"The Big Growl taught us that every dog fears something," he said gently. "I was once afraid of Trap Houses, and Fight Dogs, and losing my independence. But I also learned it's important to face your fears—to look them in the eye and challenge them. And facing my fears is how I survived and found the Pack."

"Sweet isn't afraid of anything," objected Fluff loyally.

"No, my pup. No dog is fearless. Not Storm, not Bruno, not even Snap or Mickey. How can any dog show courage if they're never afraid of anything? Your Mother-Dog is scared of many things, but she knows she has to be brave and *face* those things. And so must you—especially if you want to be Alphas of your own Packs one day!"

Tumble's ears pricked up at that. "I want to be Alpha one day. . . ."

"Me too!" Fluff knocked her shoulder into his.

"Perhaps you'll all be Alphas." Lucky laughed. "So, should we start practicing now?"

Storm wagged her tail and gave Lucky a nod of gratitude. *Lucky has always respected my opinions, even when we've had our differences.* His approval gave her a warm feeling of belonging all over again.

Hesitantly the pups followed as the two adult dogs led them past the pond and toward the river. Storm felt so proud of the pups as they bounced along behind her, over the field and past the edge of the woods, through the high grass where they sometimes hunted rabbits. It was the farthest they had ever been from the camp. Although the river was much smaller than the Endless Lake, they all slowed down and sniffed nervously at the soft ground under their paws as Lucky came to a halt on the sandy riverbank.

"Now, pups." Lucky turned to nuzzle the trembling little dogs. "Remember: Storm and I won't let anything happen to you, so don't fear the water. We'll be with you the whole time."

It was Tiny who crept forward ahead of the others, ducking her head and wagging her stumpy tail.

"I know that, Lucky." Her voice was small, but brave, as she tilted her little head to gaze at Storm. "Will you teach us now?"

"Tumble, that's wonderful!" exclaimed Storm, paddling at the golden pup's flank to shield him from the full strength of the current. "That's right, keep your nose clear of the water, but don't panic if a wave splashes up. Good!"

"Catch me!" yelped Nibble as her Father-Dog caught her gently in his jaws and tugged her closer to shore.

"Good job, Nibble. But don't get too overconfident!" Lucky licked her nose.

"I'm swimming!" yelped Fluff, splashing out into the deeper water.

"Hey!" Storm swam to her and herded her back toward the shallower water. "That's good, Fluff—but listen to your father! You mustn't take the River-Dog's good mood for granted."

Finding her paws in the shallows, Fluff nodded and shook her fur vigorously. "All right, Storm. But the River-Dog won't hurt us, I know it!"

Tiny sidled up to her litter-sister. Shyly she said, "You're really good at swimming, Fluff."

"You will be too, Tiny!" said Fluff reassuringly. "Don't be scared of River-Dog. She's just very big and strong, and we need to trust her."

"And *respect* her," Lucky added, laughing as he paddled to shore. "Now, stay in the shallows for a while, pups. I'm tired!"

They yapped their agreement, and, braver now, waded close to the bank. Storm watched them with amusement as Lucky came to her side, and they flopped down together on the crescent of gritty sand.

"That was a good idea, Storm," said Lucky. "You were right. And look at them now! You're a good teacher. You'll be a terrific Mother-Dog yourself someday."

"Humph." Storm wriggled a little uncomfortably. She wasn't at all sure she wanted noisy, disobedient pups of her own, however sweet. She changed the subject swiftly. "The water looks good, don't you think? Clean and clear."

"I was just thinking that," mused Lucky. "The River-Dog

doesn't look sick at all anymore. Maybe the effects of the Big Growl are fading. The Spirit Dogs are setting things right, as they always do."

Storm nodded doubtfully. "I suppose, even if they're wounded, the Spirit Dogs will always put things right in the end?"

"Yes. They always come back." Lucky laid his head on his paws and gazed sadly at his frolicking pups. He gave a deep sigh. "I'll be sorry if we have to leave this place."

"I know. It's just about perfect."

"And it's not only the place." His ears drooped. "I wish I could meet Bella's pups when they're born. At least while we're here, Bella knows where we are, and I can believe she'll come back to see me someday. If we leave, I may never meet the pups at all. I wish I'd fought harder to stop her and Arrow from leaving the Pack, Storm. If I'd known about her pups, maybe I would have."

"I wish they hadn't left, too," said Storm quietly. "Arrow was— well, he wasn't a brother to me, like Bella is your sister. But he was the only Fierce Dog I really knew, the only one I ever got to talk to. It would have been fun to see Fierce pups grow up—but this time, raised by kind parent-dogs. I'd have liked that." She sighed. "And it would have been so good for the Pack, too—to realize that it's a dog's parents and friends and Pack who make them what they are, not their Fierce Dog blood."

Lucky gave her a gentle, consoling nudge and laid his head upon her neck.

A breeze ruffled the surface of the shallows where the pups were playing. The water splashed Tiny's nose, making her jump and yap in surprise. Fluff was teaching her litter-siblings a jumping game over the tiny waves, and showing them how much fun it was to flop on their bellies in the shallows. Beside Storm, Lucky gave a gruff chuckle and lifted his head.

"We both miss Bella and Arrow," he murmured, "but it's hard to be sad here and now, Storm. Look at them: We've taught them how to trust the River-Dog again."

As Storm watched him watching the pups, she felt a warmth that had nothing to do with the Sun-Dog's rays. Lucky was right. Their Pack was still in danger, but they had faced danger before. Lucky and his pups were still in trouble, but she was determined to make sure they had a future.

CHAPTER FOUR

"I want you to take charge of the first hunt today, Storm." Alpha's tail swished as she walked up to the den entrance. "The prey pile has been running low, so we'll need you to bring back plenty of food."

Storm scrambled to her feet, blinking in the Sun-Dog's light. "Of course, Alpha! I've been looking forward to a hunt."

"I'll send some of our strongest hunters with you." Alpha touched her nose to Storm's. "You're more than capable of leading them. Moon and Chase will go with you to scout, and, let's see . . ." The swift-dog looked around the glade, and her eyes fell on Bruno, who lay in the sun, talking with Breeze. The brown Fight Dog looked happy as he spoke, and Breeze was nodding, her eyes soft. But they were instantly alert at Alpha's bark.

"Breeze, Bruno! I'm sending out a hunting patrol."

Both dogs got eagerly to their paws and bounded across to

Storm and Alpha; Chase and Moon were already on their way over from their own dens.

"Storm will lead the patrol," announced Alpha as the hunt-dogs gathered around.

No dog spoke. Despite how kind her Packmates had been lately, Storm felt a flicker of anxiety as she met their eyes. They were all watching her with keen anticipation. There wasn't a trace of resentment in any dog's gaze, and Bruno looked positively enthusiastic about following her lead. Once again a wave of quiet happiness rippled through her. *Things have changed so much lately.*

She couldn't repress a happy bark. "All right. Let's go! We've got work to do!"

Storm led her patrol out of the glade and through the forest, enjoying the softness of moss and grass beneath her paw pads, and the cool breeze that brought with it a tantalizing promise of prey. Tree Flower was drawing to an end, warming into Long Light, and the forest was alive with the rustle of prey. Storm licked her jaws in anticipation.

"Let's split up into smaller groups," she told the others. "There's so much prey, that will maximize our chances. Bruno and Chase, why don't you head to the hunting meadow below the cliffs?"

"Sounds good to me," growled Bruno, and the two dogs veered off.

"He didn't even argue," marveled Moon as she watched Bruno and Chase disappear into the long grass. The three female dogs padded on through trees bright with new green and yellow foliage, their paws silent on fallen blossoms. "Well done, Storm!"

"It seems like Bruno's not suspicious of you anymore," said Breeze. She looked cheerful as she sniffed the wind. "I'm really glad—there's a much happier atmosphere in the camp now!"

"I'm glad too," said Storm softly. "It does make life a lot more peaceful."

"And that's good for the pups," agreed Breeze. "Oh, what a beautiful day for a hunt!"

Storm gave a soft growl of agreement. There couldn't be a more pleasant way to spend the hours of the Sun-Dog's journey: padding quietly through the forest, noses twitching and ears pricked in concentration. For a while there was a companionable silence between the three Packmates as they focused on their search.

"Oh!" exclaimed Breeze. "Did I scent a rabbit just now?"

"I did, too." Storm halted and sniffed the wind. The rabbit scent was mingled with something meatier.

Deer!

"Moon, you go after those. Breeze, you can help Moon drive the rabbits, but keep scouting between the groups, too—you never know what else might pop up. Meanwhile, I'll check out that deer scent. If I catch sight of anything, I'll call you back—it might take a few of us to bring one down, but it would be more than worth it."

Moon gave her an approving growl and a nod, and set off after the rabbits, with Breeze in tow. Every dog was listening to Storm's orders, and she felt her heart beat with a fierce pride.

I think Alpha knew how well this would go; she must have known about Bruno's apology, too. What a wise leader she is—and kind, too. She knows I needed this.

There was a little nibble of guilt in her belly, though. Storm was aware she had more than one reason for choosing the deer scent for herself. *If I can get a sign, just an inkling that the Golden Deer is nearby . . .*

She shook herself. *Stop dreaming, Storm, and start hunting!*

A warm, rich odor clung to a tussock of grass at her shoulder. Storm hesitated, snuffling at it, filling her nostrils. Not the Golden Deer, with its particular, unique spiciness; but the scent definitely spoke of deer, and made her mouth water. Casting around for the strongest trail, Storm found a promising direction and followed it, muzzle close to the ground.

It led her across the meadow, the trail strong and easy to follow until it dispersed among a cluster of cottonwood trees. Storm walked between their smooth silver trunks, keeping her head low and her paws quiet. Above her the new leaves fluttered, casting strange dappled shadows, but the paleness of the foliage made it simple to spot the group of dark, moving shapes where the trees were thickest.

There was a clump of goat's beard growing between the trees, its tall plumes of feathery flowers making good cover. Storm slunk in among the plants and lay low, watching the deer. Their odor was very strong now, and she was downwind and perfectly placed. Could she even take one of them down alone? *Just one . . .*

Or perhaps she should be patient and follow the original plan. She could track the herd, then go back for the others—who must have caught some small prey by now—and then they might have a chance to catch two deer. *Two deer would feed the Pack for days,* she thought hungrily.

The peace in the little copse was deep and blissful, broken only by the rustling of breeze-blown leaves and the contented munching of browsing deer. So it chilled Storm's spine when a searing howl echoed across the grass.

The deer bolted instantly, their hooves a light thunder on the soft grass. Breathless and afraid, Storm leaped to her paws. The howling was too high-pitched and wild for her to identify the voice, but it was undoubtedly a dog, in pain and terrified. That dog needed help. There was no question of not responding.

Bounding out of the goat's-beard bush, she veered through the tree trunks and raced across the grassy meadow. Her thoughts tumbled over one another even as she sprinted, desperate to reach the distressed dog. *We should never have split up. We still have an enemy, and that bad dog is still among us!*

Oh, Sky-Dogs, I hope I'm not too late—

She plunged into another thickly wooded patch of forest, nearly tumbling over in her speed. The howling was closer now. *It's Moon!*

The deer-scent in her nostrils had been overwhelmed by the reek of rabbit, so she knew she was on the right track. But that scent in turn was abruptly swamped by the pungent, pervasive odor of wild garlic. It seemed to fill Storm's whole skull, making her eyes water and her nose sting. Her sense of smell was useless now—she could only strain her ears forward and crane them to the side, hunting for clues, trying to home in on the source of the howling.

She was so busy listening, focused on the terrible cries, that she almost careered into the steep hollow that opened before her paws. Scrabbling to a halt just in time, she stood on the edge, surrounded by a thick tangle of tough grass and more pungent wild garlic. Panting, Storm stretched out her neck and peered down the slope. It was almost vertical, a hidden trap for any unwary dog.

"Moon!" she barked. She could make out Moon's black-and-white fur through the undergrowth; the Farm Dog was sprawled at the foot of the sharp drop. *"Moon!"*

The pale shape moved, struggling to rise. Heart in her throat, Storm watched as Moon got gingerly to her paws, head hanging down. At least she had stopped howling, but there was still shock and pain in her blue eyes.

Moon tilted her head up, meeting Storm's frightened stare.

"Moon, are you badly hurt? What happened?"

The Farm Dog lifted a paw, wincing in agony. Next to her, Storm could make out a dead rabbit, its head and flank patched with blood. All around Moon were scattered rocks, some larger than a dog's head. They were smeared with fresh earth.

Those rocks have only just fallen!

"Moon, are you all right?" she barked again, torn with anxiety.

Moon gave a low growl, one that swelled with anger till it was almost a howl again.

"No, Storm, I'm *not* all right." Moon's white muzzle curled back to show angry fangs. "I've just been attacked!"

CHAPTER FIVE

"Hold on, Moon. We'll get you out of there." Storm crouched at the edge of the drop, pricking her ears forward and peering over. It was a horribly long drop—Moon hadn't been badly hurt, but that must have been by pure luck. If she'd fallen another way, the fast-running hunt-dog might have broken her neck.

Was she pushed? Is there an enemy nearby? Storm gave a few rapid, loud barks of summons, then turned back to her friend. "What happened, Moon?"

"It was a stupid accident," growled Moon, pawing awkwardly at the dead rabbit. "I was so focused on tracking this rabbit, but I couldn't rely on my nose because of the stench of that wild garlic up there. I had to keep my *eyes* on the wretched creature. So I never saw the land fall away."

"It could happen to any dog," Storm told her, relieved. "I can't smell a thing, either. You were lucky you weren't knocked out, and that you could howl. I came as soon as I could."

"Oh, you weren't the first," snarled Moon.

Storm flinched back, startled. *No, I got here ahead of the others—wait! Moon said she was attacked.* "What do you mean?"

"I tried to climb out of here at first, but it was hopeless. Too steep, and the slope is crumbly. I knew I'd have to howl for help, so I did—and some dog came, all right. Some dog came, saw me down here, and dislodged these rocks to topple them onto me!"

Storm felt her heart thunder against her ribs. *What? Is the traitor here, now?*

She glanced around and spotted a crumbling overhang a little to their right. It wouldn't be hard to loosen stones from there and send them tumbling down on a dog lying below, as helpless as a wounded deer.

Storm's stomach plummeted, but she also felt a throb of excitement. Moon was all right, and perhaps she had seen the traitor!

"Who, Moon?" she asked breathlessly. "Who did this?"

"I don't know!" Moon gave a strangled howl of frustration. "I couldn't see from here. The dog was nothing but a shadow. But that . . . that *creature* shoved the rocks down deliberately—that much I *do* know!"

Storm tried to beat down her disappointment. The priority here was to get Moon out of her predicament. "You're lucky you weren't killed. Can you walk?"

Moon staggered to her paws and gingerly tested her weight. "Nothing's broken, I don't think. Just bruised."

"You'll be fine," Storm reassured her. *It could have been much worse.* "Where *are* the others?"

Pawsteps and harsh panting echoed abruptly at her ear, and Storm jumped back in shock. When she turned, Bruno, Breeze, and Chase were at her side, out of breath from running, their eyes full of panic. *Of course I didn't smell them coming,* she realized, annoyed at herself. *It's that Earth-Dog-cursed garlic.*

"What happened?" barked Bruno.

"It's fine," Storm reassured him, gesturing to the precipice with her nose. "Moon fell, but she's not badly hurt."

"No thanks to that traitor dog!" barked Moon angrily from below them. "I thought our territory had been cleared, but the bad dog has struck again! I could have been *killed.*"

Chase gave a sharp yelp of horror, while Bruno looked shocked into silence, and Breeze growled in appalled dismay. "How did it happen?"

"Moon fell by accident—but then a dog pushed those rocks

over on top of her." Storm stood back to let her three Packmates peer over the edge. "We can't worry about that right now, though. We have to get her out."

"How can we pull her up from all the way down there?" Bruno's eyes were wide and afraid.

"We don't have to." Storm scratched experimentally at the steep ground. "Look, the earth is crumbling. I'm sure it can be loosened. We'll dig until the slope's shallow enough for Moon to climb."

"Good thinking," yapped Chase, and she set to work. The others joined her, scraping and digging, kicking the loose earth away with their hindpaws.

It was tougher than Storm had expected. All four dogs were soon panting hard, and their progress was slow. Below them, Moon scraped weakly at the foot of the drop, doing her best to help. Storm's paw pads ached; she could feel stinging scratches on them from the dry, stony ground, and she could hear Bruno's harsh, exhausted breathing at her ear, but at last the slope was excavated enough.

"Try now, Moon," barked Storm. "Breeze, Chase—give her a helping paw."

Moon took a determined breath. Scrambling and scrabbling,

she hauled herself up, slipping now and again despite the dogs supporting her flanks. At last, Chase and Breeze got her to the rim of the hollow, and Moon flung herself over it with a last desperate gasp.

The white-and-black dog stood trembling for a moment, her flanks heaving, as the other four dogs licked her face and shoulders. "Well done, Moon," murmured Breeze, nuzzling her.

"Well done, all of *you*," Moon said. "I just wish I'd been able to *see that dog!*"

Storm turned and studied the land around them. The overhang didn't look particularly unstable, and there was no better time than the present to investigate. She began to climb up toward its jutting tip.

"Hurry, Storm," Moon growled, an edge of panicked anger in her voice. "I want to find any clues that might tell us who pushed those rocks down."

"Storm will find anything there is to find." Breeze looked anxiously toward Storm, who nodded. "But, Moon, your legs are unsteady. Lean on my shoulder and we'll start back to camp."

Moon's breathing was still harsh and rapid, but Breeze's words seemed to calm her. She nodded. "All right, Storm. Go ahead and investigate. But I want to hear about anything you find." She propped her shoulder against Breeze's, and together the two female dogs began their slow trek back in the direction of the camp.

Storm watched them go, then turned and continued toward the overhang, her heart beating hard. She placed her paws carefully as she climbed up the bare rock. It was solid, and no dislodged stones rattled down beneath her treads. She scented the air and the rock, but once again, all smells were smothered by another odor—one that didn't belong there.

Storm edged out more confidently onto the jutting rock's flat top and gaped at the shocking mess that had been left on the overhang's surface. The hollow, raw gaps where the loosened stones had been: Those she was expecting. More surprising were the ragged plant stalks that had been torn up by the roots and strewn around.

Wild garlic.

The uprooted plants hadn't grown here, on the bare rock. The traitor had dug them up, brought them up here, and scattered and trampled them all across the jutting overhang, and the reason was obvious: Storm could detect no trace of the bad dog's scent. She growled angrily at the coldhearted deception.

One thing's for sure: This was a trap. A planned, deliberate, cruel attack. The culprit thought it through.

Whoever had covered the camp in rabbit blood, whoever had hidden savage shards of clear-stone in the prey—the same warped, calculating mind had devised this trap. Her anger turning to fear, Storm shuddered.

Below, Chase and Bruno were staring up at her, blinking against the sunlight. Storm shook herself and trotted back down to join them.

"Come on," she said in a low voice. "We'll catch up with Breeze and Moon. There's nothing to be discovered up there."

"What about the hunt?" whined Chase.

"It's more important to get back and tell Alpha about this." Storm set off toward the glade. "The forest will wait for us, and so will the prey. But the traitor could strike again at any moment."

Is Alpha ever going to stop that furious pacing? wondered Storm. Agitated, the swift-dog strode one way and then the other, over and over again, her thin tail lashing. "This is terrible news, Storm," she said at last. "I thought perhaps our troubles were finished. I thought it too soon."

Storm didn't respond.

I hoped so too. But I never really believed it. I only wish that knowing something like this would happen meant I could have stopped it! The injustice of it made her want to howl. What good was it being aware of the danger they were in if she couldn't do anything about it?

At last, Alpha came to a halt and gave a sharp bark. "Beta! Third Dog! To me."

Twitch and Lucky had been hovering nearby, aware that something was very wrong, and they bounded quickly across to their leader. Their eyes darkened and their tails stilled as they listened to Alpha retell Storm's story. By the end, when Alpha fell silent, they were exchanging glances full of fear and fury.

"This can't go on," said Twitch softly.

Lucky nodded in agreement. "Alpha, I think we need to hear everything that today's hunters can tell us. Let's find out what the others in the party have to say—they might have noticed something strange, even if they didn't realize it at the time."

"A good idea, Beta." Alpha turned her slender head and barked, "Chase! Bruno! Breeze! To me, now."

Storm felt a small wrench of unease in her gut. She didn't want all the hunters to fall under suspicion. This had been her hunt, her responsibility; the thought of more trouble and resentment stirring in the Pack as a result of her patrol was horrible. *Oh, I hope Alpha doesn't start throwing accusations. . . .*

But her anxiety turned quickly to resentment. As Alpha finished asking her questions and pricked an ear, Chase took a pace forward.

"The trouble is, none of us saw anything, Alpha." She lowered her head respectfully. "Maybe if Storm hadn't split us up and sent us in different directions—"

"Hey!" protested Storm. "We agreed on that tactic!"

Chase gave her a sidelong look, not quite meeting her eyes. "Well, you *were* the one who sent Moon after the rabbits. . . ."

Storm stiffened, feeling a growl rise in her throat. "I don't like what you're implying, Chase."

"Wait." Breeze stepped between them. "Storm didn't know the hollow was there. None of us did! And you know, maybe it was actually an accident—"

Moon gave a furious snarl, and Breeze shrank back. "Are you calling me a liar, Breeze? I'm sick and tired of not being believed! It's like being accused of prey-stealing all over again—which I *still* didn't do, by the way!"

"Stop, stop." Twitch limped forward on his three legs to touch his nose gently to Moon's, then to Breeze's. "No dog is being accused of anything, Moon." He nuzzled Storm, including her in his conciliatory words. "We're just trying to work out exactly what happened, and when. Now isn't the time for us to turn against each other. It's more vital than ever for the Pack to stay friends—to stay loyal to one another. It seems to me that this infighting is exactly what the traitor dog is trying to provoke."

Alpha nodded. "Wise words as usual, Twitch. Storm, Moon: He's right. There are no accusations here, believe me."

Tipping her head back, she let out a short, summoning howl and waited as the Pack hurried to gather around her. She gave each dog a long, steady gaze as they waited expectantly.

She cleared her slender throat. "Pack, I have something to say; and please don't think I suspect any particular one of you of being responsible for the terrible things that have happened lately. That's important."

As their tails twitched and they gave hesitant nods, Alpha raised her head. "We thought our troubles were over and that the traitor had left our territory. But today Moon was attacked when she was outside of camp on a hunt. A dog she didn't see pushed rocks on her from above, hurting her." There were whimpers of dismay from the gathered Pack, and Alpha growled them into silence and continued. "Since we don't know who did this, we can't punish any dog. But we can try to keep ourselves safe. When any of us are outside the camp, we must stay in pairs. That will be the rule from now on. It's only sensible for every dog to have another who can vouch for them. Not to keep an eye and a nose on them—I want to emphasize that—but simply to be relied on as a witness. I wish this wasn't necessary." Alpha shook her head sadly. "But as much as we all hoped it were otherwise, it seems our Pack's troubles aren't over. Not yet. But with caution and sense, we can prevent another dog from being harmed. Be careful, my Pack, and be safe. That's all."

Every dog padded away, looking reassured and somewhat mollified. *Every dog,* realized Storm with a sinking heart, *except for Moon.* There was fiery resentment in the hunter's eyes as she slunk toward her den, and Storm hurried to catch up and walk at her side.

They walked together in silence till they reached the entrance to Moon's den, then sat down. Hesitantly Breeze and Chase joined them, glancing at Storm for her approval. Storm nodded silently, though she could feel the hair on her hide rise with the force of anger emanating from Moon.

"You're not happy, Moon." Storm licked her chops, feeling like a fool as soon as the words were out. *Of course she's not happy! Her face is as dark as the Sky-Dogs before a thunderstorm.*

Moon growled under her breath. "I respect Alpha, of course I do. I wouldn't ever speak ill of her, but . . . Storm, what is she actually going to *do* about the traitor? We're all supposed to watch each other—what use is that? It just makes every dog suspicious, and the bad dog isn't stupid enough to make a move while it's being watched!"

"It's a difficult situation for Alpha," began Breeze lamely. "I know she tries. . . ."

"She's our Alpha! She's there to do difficult things, make hard decisions!" Moon lay down, head on her paws, glowering at the forest. "The traitor targeted me, Storm. Those rocks were pushed down *after* I howled for help. The bad dog knew who I was, which means they *wanted* to hurt me!"

Storm swiveled an ear toward Moon and widened her eyes. "What, Moon? Say that again. They heard you howl, identified you, and *then* they loosened the rocks?"

"Loosened them, and shoved them down on me," snapped Moon.

"So the bad dog knew it was you, specifically. You weren't visible from atop the overhang—I had to lean out over the edge just to get a glimpse—so they must have recognized your voice."

"That's what I'm saying." Moon's lip curled. "Between this, and framing me for prey-stealing—whoever the traitor is, they've got it in for me, Storm."

"Moon, I know it must have been terrifying," said Chase soothingly, "but the truth is, the whole Pack is being targeted. Maybe it's just bad luck that you've had the worst experiences. No, don't snarl at me like that! I'm just trying to make you feel better. It could honestly be a case of being in the wrong place at the wrong time."

Moon subsided with a sigh, though the snarl still lingered on her lips. "Maybe," she grunted.

Giving her a lick, Storm got to her paws and padded off, absorbed in thought. *Maybe Chase is right,* she thought. *But it does seem like a nasty coincidence. Maybe, in Moon's case, it's more than simple bad luck. . . .*

Her paws splashed in something cold and wet, and she gave a yelp of surprise. Preoccupied with the Pack's dilemma, she hadn't realized she'd paced as far as the pond. Storm blinked, then gazed down at the play of sunlight on the gentle ripples. As the water grew still again, her own reflection gazed back at her, troubled.

The dogs who had suffered at the paws of the traitor: Did they have anything in common? Storm wondered. Was there something particular about them that attracted the bad dog's malice?

If she couldn't work out the traitor's motive, how could she possibly work out who it was?

And far more important, she thought with anguish: *How can I even begin to figure out how to stop them?*

How can I find the bad dog—before something even more tragic happens to the Pack?

CHAPTER SIX

Storm scrambled to her paws, filled with resolution. *For once, I'm not a suspect. Alpha and Beta both trust me now—perhaps they'll start listening to me. I bet Alpha hasn't thought about who the bad dog is targeting. I have to bring it to her; maybe she'll have noticed something else I've missed.*

The Sun-Dog was loping down toward the tops of the trees that surrounded the camp, his light slanted and golden the way it was whenever evening drew near. Storm paused to stretch, enjoying the late warmth. *It's always good when the Sun-Dog begins to linger longer, when Ice Wind is finally long gone. It's not all bad omens these days; we just have to get through this awful time with the Pack intact. We can't lose any more dogs.*

Storm let herself yawn widely, blinked, and caught sight of Twitch.

Her ears pricked up, and she trotted over to him. She liked

their gentle, three-legged Third Dog; and didn't every dog trust him? "Twitch, can I talk to you?"

He glanced over at her, his tail wagging in welcome. "What can I do for you, Storm?"

"I'm going to talk to Alpha. Will you come with me?" After all, Twitch was one of the other dogs most affected by the traitor's attacks.

He nodded solemnly, his eyes warm. "Of course I will!"

Together they approached Alpha and Lucky's den; Storm felt somehow stronger with Twitch at her side. He was such a level-headed, kind dog, and she felt a sudden fierce need to protect him from the traitor. She had to protect *every* dog; this was her Pack, and a Pack Dog was what she was, right down to her claw-tips. *I won't let the bad dog win.*

Alpha and Lucky were relaxing at the mouth of their den, but Storm could see the alert twitch of their ears, the narrow keen-ness of their eyes. They looked protective and anxious as the pups romped and played, and Storm missed their simple, fond joy in the pups' antics—a carefree pleasure that she'd seen only the day before.

Curse that bad dog, Storm thought angrily.

Alpha and Lucky listened patiently as Storm talked about her certainty that there must be some logic behind which dogs the traitor targeted. *They're taking me more seriously because Twitch is here,* she thought, and was glad she had asked him to come along.

When she had said her piece, Alpha licked her chops thoughtfully and gave her Beta a swift glance. Lucky nodded, almost imperceptibly.

"Storm, we share your worries," said Alpha, frowning. "Somehow this situation is more frightening because we have no clues; we don't know where to begin. But you seem to have given this a lot of thought, so tell me: Do you have *any* theories about the culprit?"

"I . . . I'm not sure," sighed Storm, sitting back on her haunches. "I'm sorry, Alpha. I can't think which of us would do these things. But I have thought about who it *can't* be."

"Go on," Twitch encouraged her.

Storm took a deep breath. "Well, I think we need to look at which dogs the bad dog is targeting. There might be some reason for it we can't see yet. For instance, Moon has been attacked, so it isn't her—and there's no way Thorn and Beetle would put their own Mother-Dog in such danger." *Or frame her for a theft she didn't carry out,* she thought inwardly, but it didn't seem right to mention that aloud when it was Alpha who had punished Moon for it.

Today's incident with the rocks was proof enough.

"I agree," said Alpha, her expression inscrutable. "Are there any more?"

Storm nodded to the Third Dog. "Not Twitch, obviously; he was badly hurt when the prey was sabotaged. He wouldn't do that to himself. Not either of you two," she added in an embarrassed mumble, half glancing at Alpha and Lucky. "You wouldn't hurt your own Pack."

Alpha gave a soft laugh. "Don't be ashamed to include us, Storm. You're right, of course, we wouldn't hurt our own Pack—but we have to consider every dog's motives, just to be certain. Go on."

"Breeze is out of the question; she was with your pups when the rabbit blood was scattered over the camp. And . . . there's me. I haven't any proof, but *I* know it isn't me." Storm raised her head with nervous defiance.

Alpha nodded thoughtfully, looking very serious. "It narrows it down a little, doesn't it?"

"I suppose so," growled Storm. "But beyond that—I just don't know. I can't imagine any of the rest of our Packmates behaving this way. What possible reason would they have? I just wish we knew *why* all of this is happening. It seems like there must be some logic behind which dogs have been targeted."

"But what could the connection be?" Lucky asked thoughtfully. "The dogs who have been hurt . . . besides Moon and Twitch, there was Whisper. . . ."

Twitch shuddered at the mention of the murdered dog, his eyes sad. "Bella was the worst affected when the prey pile was poisoned," he remembered.

And then there's me.

Storm's stomach gave a sickening lurch. If specific dogs were being targeted, then she was one of them. Always, when something bad happened to the Pack, Storm had come under suspicion. Every single crime that had been committed was one it looked like Storm could have been responsible for; she'd always been alone, so she never had proof of where she had been and what she was doing.

And why would I? I don't know when the attacks are going to happen; if I knew that, I'd be the bad dog myself. If I had a witness, I'd be in the clear.

She hesitated, unwilling to share this realization. You could *see* a dog being poisoned, or pelted with rocks—being turned into a suspect was just as hurtful, but it was invisible. What if the others didn't agree?

Before she could speak again, Alpha was shaking her head

71

doubtfully. "I agree that there must be some connection, but I don't know what it could be. Whisper, Bella, Moon, Twitch . . . all these dogs came from different Packs, originally. They're hunters and Patrol Dogs and scouts. Except for being part of this Pack, I don't see what they have in common."

Storm felt her shoulders droop sadly. "Neither do I," she said. "I wish I did."

"Don't worry. And don't ever feel like you can't come to me with your thoughts, Storm," Alpha told her gently but firmly. "We have to be able to talk about this, to discuss it, or we'll never move any further forward. I think you're right: We have to do our best to work out who else it *can't* be. It's the only way we'll ever discover who it really *is*."

Storm sagged with relief. *Alpha and Lucky are taking me seriously. That has to be good.* She shivered. *I can't bear the thought of finding out one of my Packmates did this—but we must find the bad dog.*

Lucky was staring straight ahead, his yellow tail thumping in a slow rhythm. "It's hard to take in," he murmured. "Rake, Ruff, Woody, and Dart are long gone, just like Bella and Arrow. I doubt very much they'd come back to our territory just to do this, to hurt us. And the dogs who are still here . . . it's not that I don't take you seriously, Storm," he added hurriedly, "but it's a lot for any dog to contemplate. Little Sunshine, a killer? Or Daisy?" He licked his chops. "Bruno? He might be surly sometimes, but he has never been anything but loyal to the Pack. The same goes for Snap. Mickey—no, I just don't believe he's capable of it. Chase? I don't know her as well as I know the others, but I've been Pack-mates with her long enough—and I know she's a good dog, a good *Pack Dog*. I know it in my bones."

"That's the trouble," sighed Alpha. "We only have our bones to go on, and that hasn't helped us so far."

Storm's head dipped. Well, what had she expected? That Alpha or Beta would have instant, easy answers? Maybe deep down, she actually *had* thought that.

No. Be sensible, Storm, she scolded herself, *and take this problem one bite at a time.* She'd decided to talk to her Alpha, and she'd done it, and that had been the right thing to do. Now, at least, she knew she wasn't the only dog gnawing over the mystery.

But she knew she couldn't leave it like this; she couldn't just drop all the responsibility at Alpha's den mouth like an unwanted chunk of rabbit. As Storm padded away from the leaders' den, she felt her muscles tense with determination.

I can't just wait around, wondering if Alpha's come to any conclusions. What if another dog gets hurt in the meantime? I need to take action, protect the Pack—even if that means nothing more than talking things over with my Packmates.

The dogs who had been targeted were the ones least likely to be guilty—so she should talk with them. There was a chance they'd seen something—something that was significant, but they didn't realize it at the time. And it might be hard for dogs to think about the attacks—and the chance there might be more—but discussing it openly might actually make them just a little safer. They'd be on the alert—and that felt like the most useful thing Storm could do for them right now.

A dark-brown shape was heading for the camp border at the edge of the glade, about to vanish among the tree trunks. Storm gave a soft bark.

"Breeze! Wait."

The brown dog turned to give Storm a quizzical look over her shoulder. "What is it, Storm? I'm supposed to meet Daisy to patrol."

"I'll be quick." Storm swallowed. "It's just—I need to talk to you. About the bad dog."

Breeze's brow furrowed. "The bad dog? Why would you want to talk to *me* about that?"

"I'm sure the traitor will strike again, Breeze. It's awful to think about, but I believe we have to. It's the only way to ensure that we might be ready for another attack." Storm licked her jaws. "I've been trying to work out which dogs *didn't* do these things. Right now, that's easier than trying to imagine which dog is actually capable of them."

"What's your best guess at the moment, Storm?" Breeze asked. She sat back on her haunches, tilting her head curiously.

"I think we can eliminate the dogs who have been targeted . . . Twitch, Moon, Bella, and . . . well, clearly Whisper is out of the question." Storm felt a stab of grief at the mention of poor Whisper, and she shivered. "And I know you were with the pups when the camp was polluted with that blood. But the trouble is, it could be *any* other dog."

Breeze shuddered. "Sky-Dogs," she whispered softly. "I can't bear to think about it."

"But we have to," Storm pointed out. "And I know you observe the camp a lot, while you're taking care of the pups, and—well, I suppose I'm asking if you've seen anything?"

"Like what?" Breeze twitched her ears forward, looking puzzled.

"That's the trouble, I don't *know*," exclaimed Storm in frustration. "Just something unusual: maybe a dog who seemed to be in the wrong place . . . something that seemed normal at the time, but looking back it was . . . just not quite right. Out of character."

"Oh. I do see what you're nibbling at." Breeze's eyes narrowed in concentration. "Truly, Storm? I can't think of anything. There hasn't been anything . . . well, *strange* that I've noticed around camp lately. No dogs behaving oddly or differently, nothing like that."

"Oh," sighed Storm. "Well, it was worth asking."

"Of course it was," Breeze told her. "And I'll be even more watchful now, I promise. We all have to stay alert. If anything strange happens, I'll tell you at once."

Storm nodded, suddenly feeling unbearably tired. "Thanks, Breeze."

"It's nothing. Now, why don't you go to your den?" Breeze nuzzled Storm's neck fondly and gave her ear a lick. "You've had a tough day. Maybe things will look clearer in the morning, after a good night's sleep."

"You're probably right." Storm touched noses with the gentle-eyed dog. "Good night. And thanks."

Breeze padded off into the trees, and Storm trudged to her den. Her legs suddenly ached with weariness, and she sank gratefully onto her bedding. She expected to drop off instantly, but sleep evaded her like a dodging, darting squirrel.

Her mind clawed at the mystery of the bad dog, and her eyes kept flicking open. However much she tossed and turned, and dragged her bedding into new positions, she just could not drift into blissful unconsciousness.

What if it isn't only one dog? she asked herself, even as she squeezed her eyes shut and willed sleep to come. *Maybe there's more than one traitor.*

Could it really be one—or more—of my dearest friends?

Opening her eyes again, Storm stared miserably at the exposed roots that poked through her den wall. Daisy was such a sweet-natured dog, brave and kind. And she was *small* . . . not that size always mattered, if a dog could catch an enemy unawares.

Mickey was a big dog, but his mild nature made him an even less likely culprit than Daisy. Snap or Bruno? Snap was quick and cunning, and Bruno was certainly fierce and burly enough to take down most dogs. But despite her differences with both of them, Storm couldn't believe it of either Snap or Bruno.

The least likely bad dog of all was Sunshine. She was little—but like Daisy, that didn't have to matter. *She still has teeth.* Storm's mind recoiled from the idea. Sunshine had always seemed so happy to be Omega; she was more content than any dog in the Pack, as if she'd found true meaning in her life.

But what if she wasn't happy with it anymore? Could the little dog be simmering with resentment beneath it all? Had she secretly rebelled at her status, at having to make do with the last and smallest prey every night?

It was no use; sleep wouldn't come. Staggering to her paws, Storm slunk from her den and walked in a daze around the camp's border. The night was clear and starlit, the sky still dark blue rather than black, the air fresh with the scents of oncoming Long Light. But as she paced, she realized the stars were vanishing one by one, beginning at the horizon; light rain began to speckle her coat. Storm craned her head to peer at the sky. Clouds had obliterated the stars, and the raindrops were cold despite the change of season. She gave a long sigh and trudged on, sniffing dutifully at the border as she walked.

The rain was falling harder now; her fur clung to her skin, heavy with wetness. The clouds seemed to be thickening rather than clearing, and something in the atmosphere made the hairs on her spine lift. Glancing up again at the sky, she saw Lightning Dog race in an instant from the clouds to the earth. In his wake came the thundering rumble of the Sky-Dogs; they always seemed to chase Lightning when he sprinted, just for fun.

Her eyelids felt impossibly heavy. *I might sleep now.* Storm padded back to her den, tail drooping and dripping; she didn't even have the energy to shake herself. Curling up on her soft mossy bedding—*Sunshine brought this for me; how could she be bad?*—Storm was at last overwhelmed by a long, dark, and dreamless sleep.

Storm had no idea how long she'd slept. She was jerked into wakefulness by a terrible, wailing howl that made her clench her teeth.

The Sun-Dog is up and running—it's morning. She shook herself, stumbling a little as a fog of drowsiness clung to her.

The high howl came again, splitting the air—a horrible sound of grief and desperation. Now Storm was fully awake. Tightening her jaws, she sprang out of her den and raced toward the source of the dreadful noise.

She wasn't alone; alongside her ran Snap, Breeze, and Mickey. Moon hurtled from her den and joined them.

"What's happening?" cried Sunshine, frozen in terror as they passed her. "What's wrong?"

"Who knows?" barked Snap.

"It's coming from High Watch!" gasped Mickey.

Chase bolted out from the trees and ran with them. Sunshine took off in pursuit, small legs a blur beneath her shaggy white coat, but she was soon left behind. Alpha sprang from her den, and when the pups tried to follow, Lucky summoned them back with a bark that was not to be argued with. He shielded the little dogs with his body as he stared after his running Pack.

Storm's heart thundered as she saw Alpha first catch the leading dogs, then streak ahead. She was so fast! Alpha raced up the winding path to High Watch. The track underpaw was slippery with mud after the heavy rain, and all the dogs stumbled and slithered as they followed, leaving deep claw marks in the loose, wet earth.

The line of Packmates was much more strung out by the time Alpha leaped up the last rocky ledge to the cliff top and vanished over it. Storm was only a few paces behind her, though, and with one bound she was on the plateau and sprinting after her leader. The pounding steps of her Packmates echoed behind her, one by one, as they too reached the summit.

Not again, Storm kept thinking. *Please not again. Let it be an accident. Let it just be that the High Watch dog has gotten caught in thorns—who's on High Watch, anyway?*

Cold terror swept through her lungs and belly as she remembered. *Daisy!*

Alpha skidded to a halt on the damp grass ahead of her, and Storm almost collided with the swift-dog. Mickey, Snap, Breeze, and Chase were at their side in an instant, but Storm didn't turn to look at them: She felt a rush of pure relief. In front of Alpha stood Daisy, alive and well—but quivering with shock and terror. Her little head was raised to the Sky-Dogs, her jaws open wide as she howled and howled in despair.

"Daisy! *Daisy!*" commanded Alpha. "Daisy, *what is it?*"

Her sharp words finally penetrated the little dog's head. Daisy turned, eyes filled with stunned misery, and stared at her Packmates.

"Bruno . . ." From a howl, her voice had fallen to a high, tortured rasp. "It's *Bruno*. There."

Alpha stiffened, and stared past Daisy. "What?" Her voice made Storm's blood run ice-cold.

"He's dead." Daisy's voice faded, choked with horror and grief. "Bruno . . . my friend Bruno . . . He's *dead*."

CHAPTER SEVEN

"*No!*" *Mickey's agonized howl shattered the* awful silence.

Storm was frozen where she stood. She felt as if she were viewing the scene from outside—floating—watching herself and the rest of her grief-stricken, disbelieving Pack. Daisy nodded feebly at a large slab of rock near the cliff edge; Alpha's paws shook as she walked toward it. There was a dark smear of blood across the pale stone, but Bruno was mostly hidden; Storm could see only a single lifeless paw.

Snap was nuzzling her mate, Mickey, trying frantically to console him. Chase and Breeze stood flank-to-flank, dumbfounded. Moon gave a high, whimpering howl of distress; as soon as Thorn and Beetle appeared, they ran to her, licking comfortingly at her raised throat. Between the bigger dogs, a small dirty-white shape pushed through, last to arrive, panting from the exertion.

Sunshine crept closer to Daisy, her dark eyes stunned, her whole body shaking. "Is it true? Did I hear that right, Daisy? *Bruno?*"

Daisy could only nod once, miserably. Even her wiry fur seemed to droop.

Mickey shook himself violently, his jaws clenched. He took a couple of steps forward and placed his paws on either side of the two little dogs, sheltering them. Dropping his head, he began to lick their ears gently.

Those three and Bruno, they were all part of the Leashed Pack after the Big Growl, Storm realized with a wrench in her belly. *They learned to survive together, without their longpaws. They were all so close. Perhaps that shared history makes their bond even stronger than the ones between regular Pack Dogs. Does it make their grief far deeper, too?*

Storm's heart ached for them; she could not imagine how they were feeling. She hadn't known Bruno for as long as they had, but she too felt hollow with grief and shock. She and the big dog had only just started to get along like true Packmates. As Alpha stalked stiffly behind the rock slab and stared down, Storm started hesitantly toward her, Chase and Breeze at her tail.

"No," snapped Alpha, clearly and sharply. "All of you, stay back."

As they halted, she sniffed at the ground and at the covered corpse. After a long time, she raised her head and sighed deeply. She turned to her Packmates.

"Only a large, vicious animal could have killed Bruno," she said, her voice rough and raspy. "But that rain last night—it's washed away any traces. There are no paw prints. There's no scent."

"Large and vicious," growled Snap, leaving Mickey's side to take a couple of paces forward. "You mean a giantfur, maybe? A giant sharpclaw? Or . . . could it have been a dog?"

Alpha was silent for long moments, licking her chops. She glanced back at what lay behind the rock, and when she turned back to the Pack, she didn't quite meet any dog's eyes.

"Yes," she admitted at last. She sounded as if she could hardly get the words out; as if her jaws were full of poisoned prey. "Yes, it could have been a dog. I think . . . I'm almost certain . . . Yes. It was a dog."

Gasps and muffled whimpers erupted from the Pack. A low, agonized growl sounded from Mickey's throat.

Alpha drew herself up stiffly. "All of you, return to the camp. Except for you, Mickey," she added as he began to protest. "And Storm and Breeze, and Moon. You four can help me move Bruno. We can't leave him up here. We'll bury him next to Whisper."

A cold chill went through Storm's rib cage at the sound of the gray dog's name. *Whisper.*

Whisper tried to warn me!

He knew this was going to happen. My dream was clear. Perhaps I could have stopped this. . . . Perhaps I was supposed to stop this. . . .

But how could she have foreseen it? Guilt flashed through her. Bruno had been one of the Packmates she still suspected of possibly being the bad dog; could there be a worse, more tragic proof of his innocence? And who would want to hurt Bruno? He could be grumpy and abrasive, but his size and strength belied a surprising gentleness.

I didn't see it coming. But I should have. Whisper warned me. He warned me.

Mickey nudged Daisy and Sunshine with his nose and shepherded them away, muttering pointless reassurance; Daisy was still shaking as she set off back down the cliff path. The rest of the Pack followed, their tails hanging low, and Mickey stood and watched them go. His chest was heaving, Storm noticed.

Mickey's pain was awful to see. Turning tactfully away, Storm paced over to the slab of rock. For a moment she hesitated, and then she stepped around behind it.

Sky-Dogs! Storm sucked in a shocked breath.

No wonder Alpha had sent the rest of the Pack away. No dog should see this, if they didn't have to—and especially not little Sunshine. *I wish Daisy hadn't found him. She shouldn't have seen this either. . . .*

Bruno did look almost as if a giantfur had attacked him, but Storm knew why Alpha had instantly suspected a dog. The injuries were just too vicious, too *deliberate* to be the work of some raging animal.

The big dog's throat had been torn out. That was bad enough— a horrible echo of what had happened to Whisper—but far worse, his entire lower jaw had been ripped away. Blood was splashed on the rock and on the grass around him; he lay in a dark congealing lake of it. His eyes were open, glazed in death, and his expression was more one of shock than terror.

Storm took an instinctive step back. She could hardly bear to look at the evidence of poor Bruno's violent killing, but there was something even worse about the state of his body. Her stomach twisted sharply.

His jaw . . . torn right away from his skull.

Storm felt sick, her belly and fur tingling with a feeling of familiarity—but she could not put her paw on why it was so familiar. . . .

"Let's get to work," Alpha said, softly but clearly. As if a trance had broken, the other four dogs shook themselves and prepared to drag Bruno as carefully as possible down the steep and winding cliff path.

It was a long, difficult, painful task; Bruno's body was heavy and the thudding sound it made as they maneuvered him down the steeper shelves was awful. Behind them, a thin, dark smear of half-dried blood marked their path. Once they were down among the trees, the ground was at least flat, but the big dog was an awkward burden to drag through the pine trunks and the thorny scrub.

The four Packmates and their Alpha had to take frequent breaks, but at last, exhausted and panting hard, they released Bruno in the dappled light of the forest clearing. His big frame flopped to the ground, lifeless, and rolled slightly down a shallow slope.

Inwardly Storm shuddered. There was Whisper's grave, overgrown with grass and moss, dotted with tiny purple flowers. It was settling back into the paws of the Earth-Dog, just as it had been in her dream.

And now we'll dig that fresh grave. The one Whisper told me we'd dig.

They set to work, tearing and clawing at the soft earth, kicking the loosened mud aside till they had created a hollow deep enough to keep Bruno safe from surface scavengers. *Deep enough to deter foxes,* Alpha had said when they'd buried Whisper; but Whisper had been a smaller dog. It was a much bigger job to bury Bruno, but at last the hole was deep enough, and together they dragged Bruno to its edge. With a shove from Mickey and Storm, he rolled and thudded into dark, moist, exposed earth.

My paws. They're shaking. It was just exhaustion, Storm told herself, but she knew that wasn't true. It was shock and grief—and fear. *My dream. This is just like my dream.*

I didn't know I'd feel so strongly about losing Bruno. I didn't get along with him well—not till the end—and he made trouble for me. But he wasn't a bad dog. He certainly wasn't the *bad dog.*

Misery choked her. *Bruno and I had only just learned how to get along, Earth-Dog. And now he's dead, and you've taken him.*

Moon gazed down into the grave, her drooping ears pricking up suddenly with sad curiosity. "Bruno's jaw," she murmured, her eyes distant. "He looks—it looks just like what happened to Terror. Remember, Storm?"

"That doesn't mean anything." Breeze's voice held an edge as she sidled closer and pressed her flank to Storm's. "Just because it's what Storm did to that mad dog Terror—there's no way she'd do such a thing to Bruno. He was our Packmate!"

Storm felt her stomach shrink within her, and she couldn't help cringing. Breeze always meant well, but there were times Storm wished she'd keep her jaws shut. Moon was staring at Breeze, her eyes startled.

"I didn't mean that at all," Moon stammered. "You know that, Storm, don't you? It was just a . . . an observation. A big, strong dog—as big and strong *as* you—did this. That's all."

Storm nodded quickly. "I know. Of course."

But the air was suddenly crisp with unease, and Storm felt heat run through the skin beneath her fur. Moon looked guilty, Breeze exasperated, and Alpha and Mickey simply uneasy.

"We should get back to the camp soon," said Mickey, just as the silence was growing unbearable. The Farm Dog's voice still sounded hoarse and rough, and again Storm felt a sharp twist of sympathy for him. No dog liked to bury an old friend. "Come on. We have to cover him."

"Of course." Breeze nuzzled him gently. "Then he'll truly be with the Earth-Dog, Mickey."

It didn't take nearly so long to kick and scrape the soil back over Bruno's corpse. When he was hidden from sight and the earth was piled back, it made Storm feel sick with despair. *He's gone. We won't ever see him again—except, maybe, in dreams.*

The sad and silent group plodded back to the glade, each dog lost in thought. Alpha picked up her pace as they reached the camp border, and she trotted in ahead of the others, barking a summons to the whole Pack.

"Pack! To me!" She stood patiently while the dogs gathered around her. Storm couldn't help noticing that no dog's tail wagged; every Packmate stood straight, their heads high and their faces somber. "I've been giving this a lot of thought, and I have come to a decision. Since it seems obvious to me now that poor Bruno was killed by a large dog, watches will be taken only by smaller Packmates until we have dealt with this."

"But . . ." Sunshine, shivering, crept forward, her shoulders low and humble. "Alpha, us small dogs won't be any match for the bad dog, if it attacks. . . ."

Alpha closed her eyes and gave a heavy sigh. "I know, Omega. But all of us bigger dogs will be watching one another. That means the traitor won't have a chance to bother you. I hope." She licked the little dog's nose. "You're the only dogs I can afford to trust with this, Sunshine. I know you won't let me down."

Storm could only listen, her mouth dry, a hollow sensation in her stomach. *I'm the biggest dog here. And the strongest. Now that Woody has left and Bruno is dead—even* I *think I'm the most likely suspect.*

Even as the horrible thought struck her, from the corner of her eye Storm saw Snap lift her head. The smaller dog gave a whine to draw Alpha's attention.

"I hate to say this, but I'm going to. I *must*." Snap shot a glance at Storm, and Storm almost recoiled at the hostility in her eyes. Snap's hard brown stare was fixed on her, but Storm got the clear impression that Snap was talking to every dog *but* her. "The only dogs big enough to kill Bruno would be Storm and—*maybe*—Mickey or Lucky." Snap licked her jaws and narrowed her eyes. "But Mickey couldn't have done it. He was with me. And Lucky was Bruno's Packmate, for a long time. They all survived the Growl together. They were friends, we all know that."

"What are you saying, Snap?" Alpha's tone was calm and steady.

It's obvious what she's saying. Storm felt the weight of horrible inevitability pressing down on her shoulders.

Snap sat back on her haunches, looking grim. "Every dog knows that Storm hated Bruno."

The heat of rage was a physical force in Storm's chest, swamping her misery. She struggled to hold the fury back, but it was too strong. It escaped her in a violent, angry bark.

"That isn't true! I never hated Bruno! *He* hated *me*. But we made up! I wouldn't hurt him. I was *glad* that we had become friends, after everything that had happened. . . . Bruno even apologized to me!"

Chase shut one eye and swished her tail doubtfully. "That doesn't sound much like Bruno to me."

He's right. Desperately Storm turned to Lucky—but to her dismay, even the Pack Beta looked unsure. *Lucky! You were like a Father-Dog to me! How can you believe this?*

She felt as if an enormous boulder were crushing her to the ground. *I can't prove it—no one saw us talk. There's no way I can prove that Bruno said he was sorry!*

"It's true!" To Storm's surprise, it was Daisy who trotted to the center of the circle. The little dog's eyes still looked hollow and grief-stricken, but there was a determined set to her jaw.

"Bruno told me!" announced Daisy, fixing Alpha with her most resolute gaze. "We talked about it only the other day. He said he was worried, and he felt guilty—that he'd maybe been unfair to Storm."

Alpha looked startled. "Did he tell you he'd apologized to her?"

"No . . ." Daisy admitted. "He didn't say *that*. But he *was* sorry.

He told me so. And if Storm says he did, then I believe her." She turned and gazed steadily at Storm, who felt her heart turn over with gratitude.

"I agree," Sunshine piped up, wagging her ragged plume of a tail. "Storm would never hurt Bruno, anyway. I *know* she wouldn't. She's a kind, good dog!"

Alpha nodded, got to her paws, and looked around the Pack silently, as if coming to a decision. Storm waited with her heart beating high in her throat.

Alpha and Beta know me. They must know I wouldn't do this. But could she be certain? However much they cared for Storm, they hadn't done a great job of standing up for her recently.

"Storm is a member of our Pack," Alpha said at last. "A *loyal* Packmate who has stood by us in many dangers—who has fought off enemies, and *saved my pups*. I will not have the members of this Pack turning on one another; that's exactly what the traitor wants." Storm's ears pricked up with relief as Alpha's eyes grew brilliant and ferocious. "No dog is to accuse any other from now on, unless they have some proof. Wild accusations and arguments do not help the Pack, or any dog in it! Is that understood?"

Snap's head and tail drooped, and she gave a resentful growl, but she lowered her shoulders and gave a single nod. "Yes, Alpha."

She shuffled back to a dazed Mickey's side.

Warmth returned to Storm's belly and limbs. *Alpha trusts me,* she thought, *and so does Omega. And so do many dogs in the ranks between them. I don't have anything to fear from my own Pack.* The relief made her dizzy.

Chase grunted and growled. "Alpha . . . there is another dog who could have killed Bruno."

Alpha swung around sharply. "I said no wild accusations!"

"I'm not making one." Chase took a pace forward, and raised her head to stare at Alpha.

"Hush, Chase!" Breeze nudged her anxiously. "Don't say—"

"I am going to say it," she snapped at Breeze, and returned her gaze to Alpha's. "I think—it might have been the Fear-Dog."

There was a moment's shocked silence. Then Mickey gave a dark growl of derision. "There's no such thing as the Fear-Dog!"

"Exactly, Mickey." Snap barked a laugh of agreement. "And even if there was, Spirit Dogs don't go around tearing out throats. They don't bother themselves with flesh-and-blood dogs like us!"

Storm listened in silence as others in the Pack began to ridicule Chase's claim. She should have felt reassured by Mickey's scorn, by Snap's dismissal of the whole mad idea of murderous Spirit Dogs. . . .

But she wasn't nearly so sure.

My dreams. I've dreamed of the Fear-Dog; that has to mean something. Even Lucky trusts the power of dreams—after all, they showed him the Storm of Dogs long before it happened. She shuddered.

The Fear-Dog was an invention of the mad Terror—or so they'd thought. Every dog in the Pack knew the great, black, snarling Spirit Dog had just been a story that Terror had made up, to strike fear and obedience into his own cowering Pack.

But what if he's real?

When the dogs of Terror's former Pack had joined the Wild Pack, they'd brought the stories and the belief and the legend with them, the way they'd brought their own scents, their own ears and tails and paws: that was how deeply they'd believed in Terror and his fake Spirit Dog.

But what if a spirit can become *real?* wondered Storm, her gut icy-cold. *Can it be created out of stories? If enough dogs believe, does a Spirit Dog come into being?*

What if it wasn't just the stories they brought with them?

What if they brought the Fear-Dog himself?

CHAPTER EIGHT

Storm paced the camp's border, over and over again, every muscle and nerve drawn tight. Beyond the trees, the Sun-Dog was creeping below the horizon, gilding the pine trunks with his golden glow, and Storm couldn't help feeling that even he—even that great Spirit Dog—was slinking away to avoid her. Perhaps the Sun-Dog had a problem with Fierce Dogs, too? *Maybe,* thought Storm, *even the Sun-Dog is made a little nervous by the presence of such a big, ferocious—* Fierce—*dog. Perhaps he, too, rejects dogs like me. . . .*

Storm was beginning to grow very tired of all this. None of the Pack dogs would meet her eyes, however hard she glared at them. If she turned her head and caught one of them watching her, she saw only fear and suspicion in their swiftly averted faces.

Did it mean nothing when all of you began to trust me? Have you forgotten how I saved the pups? Have you forgotten I'm your loyal Packmate?

Daisy stood up for me. Sunshine did, too. And Alpha trusts me absolutely! So why can't all of you?

She turned her stare on Snap, but the hunt-dog looked sharply away, glowering at the ground. Mickey rose to his paws, looking embarrassed, but when he took a pace toward Storm, Snap muttered something that she couldn't hear. Mickey swallowed, gave Storm a hesitant, sympathetic glance, but sat back down.

Even you, Mickey? Even you?

She didn't know which feeling was stronger: the anger or the hurt. Their suspicion stung her like a swarm of bees in her belly.

It was not so long ago that they couldn't be nice enough to me. Snap brought me soft moss to lie on. And now . . . Storm growled, deep in her throat, and paced faster, breaking into a trot.

It would be best if she could tire herself out before it was time to sleep, but her brain was buzzing with resentment and fury. She couldn't imagine ever sleeping again. On she paced, walking and running around the clearing, until the Sun-Dog had vanished altogether and the Moon-Dog had risen in the gray-blue sky. *She* at least wasn't turning her face away from Storm; she shone full and round and bright on the glade, lighting every pair of suspicious eyes with her silver glow.

One by one, the Pack members were padding to the center

of the camp, gathering in their circle for the Great Howl. Storm hung back, reluctant to share space with any of them, her anger still hot in her throat.

But as they settled, sitting or lying down, giving one another friendly licks and flicking their ears as they greeted one another, Storm began to relax.

It's time for the Great Howl. The whole point is to bind us together, as a Pack. It's what the Moon-Dog wants. And it's what we need right now.

Her stiff legs trembled as she stalked forward to join the Pack. *Maybe this Howl will make everything the way it was again. Maybe this will fix things.*

Maybe this is my last chance . . . my last chance to prove I belong in this Pack.

And if I can't show them, if I can't make them believe it . . . what then? What will I do? Misery and confusion sank into Storm's bones.

She sat down, her tail curled tight against her, picking a spot where her flanks wouldn't touch any other dog. No dog moved closer to her; maybe they could feel the rage that lifted the fur of her hide. *Maybe they're afraid of me.*

Maybe they're right to be.

Storm tilted back her head to stare morosely at the Moon-Dog. Then she narrowed her eyes. There was something odd about the great silver Spirit Dog now. Her glow had dulled, and Storm wasn't the only one who had noticed it.

Around her, dogs were shifting, fidgeting, muttering. Ears were tucked tightly back, claws scraped nervously at the earth. *Is it a cloud?* wondered Storm.

But as the Moon-Dog rose higher, the cloud didn't pass. The pale disc reddened, as if it was stained with blood. Stars were blinking into life, glimmering in the darkening sky, and Storm realized suddenly: *There are no clouds.*

What's happening?

A whimper from Sunshine broke the silence. "The Moon-Dog is angry!"

Storm glanced at her, shocked. Maybe the little dog was right. When Storm turned back to the sky, the Moon-Dog's hide was not silver at all: She looked like a giant, sinister red eye, staring at the Pack with a dull, blank rage. It reminded Storm of something . . . something awful. Abruptly she realized: It looked just like the mad dog Terror's crazed glare.

A ripple of icy fear ran beneath Storm's fur, mixed with a horrible shame. *Have I caused this? Has the Pack? The things that have happened lately—have we done this to the Moon-Dog? Is she really this angry with us?*

A quivering voice broke the silence. "The Fear-Dog," whined

Breeze, crouching low to the ground. "It's the Fear-Dog."

Chase gave a low, terrified howl. "The Fear-Dog has cast his shadow over the Moon-Dog! Is he *eating* her?"

Chase and Breeze both believed firmly in the Fear-Dog, Storm remembered: They had both been members of Terror's Pack. But the others were cowering now too—even Mickey had pressed himself to the earth, trembling.

"Is it a sign?" whined Beetle. "Is something bad going to happen?"

"Quiet, now!" Alpha took a step into the circle. "There's nothing to be afraid of, my Pack. There's no such thing as the Fear-Dog!"

"Yes," whined Chase. "There is. Look at him."

"No!" barked Alpha. "That's no Fear-Dog, It's just . . ." Her voice trailed off, her ears tucked back, and her tail trembled anxiously. "It's the weather. That's all. Just the weather. Rain's coming."

But that's no cloud. Storm stared at the rust-red Moon-Dog. *There are no clouds tonight. . . .*

"I've never seen this happen before," said Moon, her eyes wide. "There's never been a cloud like that. Not ever!"

"Is it hurting the Moon-Dog?" whimpered Omega in distress.

"If that *is* the Fear-Dog, he's harming her!"

"Pack! Stop worrying." Lucky sprang forward past Alpha. "This is not the Fear-Dog!"

"I agree with Lucky," declared Twitch, stepping forward to stand beside the Pack's Beta. "This is something we haven't seen before, but it's natural. It's only a mood of the Moon-Dog." He drew a breath. "But since she's in a bad mood, maybe it's best that we don't Howl tonight."

"That's true," said Lucky. "It's clear the Moon-Dog is not herself. Alpha, do you agree?"

"Yes." Alpha nodded firmly. "Let's leave our Howl till the Moon-Dog is more kindly inclined toward all dogs. But listen to Beta and Third Dog, Packmates. There is no such thing as the Fear-Dog."

She sounds determined, thought Storm, eyeing Alpha. *She sounds convincing. But there's fear in her eyes, too. Alpha's as confused and unsure and distressed as the rest of us. . . .*

Storm swallowed hard, suddenly more afraid than ever.

"I don't know what's happening," Alpha went on, a hint of a tremor in her stern voice. "But it has nothing to do with Terror's wild stories. Go to your dens. We will leave the Moon-Dog to rest and recover; she will be our beloved Spirit Dog again soon."

One by one, the dogs rose to their paws and slunk off toward their dens, watched by that great round red eye. Around them everything seemed so still and quiet, thought Storm, as if the forest itself were afraid of the Moon-Dog tonight.

She gazed up at the great Spirit Dog in awed trepidation, feeling the dark night press in on her hide, and a violent shudder ran through her bones.

Rain. It fell in a torrent from the sky, relentless. The black downpour was so heavy it was hard to breathe, and water streamed into her eyes and nostrils.

Water? Storm wasn't sure. Was it blood, then, or only the stench of it? It seemed that blood filled her mouth and her head; it streamed into her eyes, it drenched her fur. That meant it was a dream, she was sure. Only in dreams did the sky rain blood.

And yet it felt real, all real. Blood in her eyes or not, Storm could see enough. She could see too much.

All around her, dogs were battling to the death. Fighting, biting, scratching, and snarling. Dogs collided in a mass of violent confusion, slithering in the mud. High above, the Sky-Dogs were joining in the fight; thunder crashed and rolled, and Lightning streaked across the sky in white flashes, over and over again.

Despite the chaos and the noise and the driving rain, nothing could blunt Storm's sense of smell. The stink of blood was thick on the sodden air; she tasted its rusty tang in her mouth.

Lucky and Terror were locked in combat, rolling over and over on the slippery ground, the golden dog's jaws tearing at Terror's ear. There were so many other dogs Storm knew—of course there were. She remembered this battle against Terror's Pack too well. It was real. The place and the struggle were real; the blood was real.

But why was she back here? Why was it happening again?

Bella and Martha and Moon were in the heart of the chaos, fighting with savage desperation. She could see Twitch, snarling and biting at dogs of his own former Pack; of course, this was when he had finally turned against Terror's brutal rule. But others had stayed loyal to the mad tyrant: dogs Storm now knew as friends were attacking her Pack. There were Splash, Chase, and Breeze, fighting in a frenzy. Off to her flank she saw Ruff and Rake, Whisper and Woody, their teeth snapping wildly at her Packmates.

The smell of the blood and the rage of the storm thrilled through her bones. Through the blinding rain she saw Terror throw off Lucky and charge straight toward her. She wasn't afraid. She leaped gladly to meet him, her jaws open in a snarl of fury.

I want this fight!

She crashed into Terror head-on, their jaws locking in a deadly struggle. His mad yellow-red eye glared into hers, but she wasn't scared of this brute; she bit and tore, feeling her fangs sink into his flesh.

And suddenly, horribly, her hold broke. Terror fell away, flailing and uttering a gurgling, agonized howl. His dismembered jaw was still caught between her teeth; she spat it out, tasting blood on her tongue. Her mouth was full of that dark, thick fluid.

But of course it was. She'd tasted it from the start. This was always going to happen. It was always meant to happen.

On the ground, in the sticky, sucking mud, the maimed Terror writhed and squirmed in agony, his face disfigured almost beyond recognition, his life spilling out of him. Storm felt no pity. She gazed down at the dying dog, his lifeblood filling her mouth and nostrils, seeping through every fiber of her body. Triumph surged through her, making her bones thrum with a fierce and lethal joy.

She became aware of eyes fixed on her, and she jerked her head up to look around. Dogs were staring at her, their faces full of horror and shock. And fear. Terror's Pack and her own friends: They had all gone unnaturally still, the battle forgotten, to gape at her victory. They were afraid of her; she could see it in their wide white eyes.

And between them . . . other dogs skulked. Shadow dogs, with featureless faces.

Watching her. Watching, and seeing, and knowing what she was. . . .

Storm woke with an abrupt, awful jolt. Her paws were no longer half sunk in mud; she stood on dry, dusty earth that was littered with twigs and leaves. The rushing sound of water still filled her ears, but it wasn't raining; the noise was the river, flowing only a rabbit-chase away. She stared at it in shock, watching the dance of moonlight on its surface.

I did it again. I walked in my sleep.

A sickening rush of disappointment flooded through her. *I thought it was over. I haven't sleepwalked in so long. I hoped it would never happen again.*

The dream was still vivid in her head. She could still see the horrified faces of those dogs, Terror's Pack and her own. The worst of it was, it was no dream, but a memory. It had happened; she had done that awful thing, and her feeling of triumph and delight in Terror's death had been real.

I ripped off his jaw. I remember how it tasted. It didn't disgust me: I loved that moment. It tasted . . . good. Like victory.

I remember I was glad.

And Bruno had died like that. Bruno's life had ended in just the same way as Terror's: his jaw torn savagely from his head.

The terrible things that have happened lately . . . Are they because of Terror? Has it all been about that insane dog?

The red Moon-Dog that rose tonight had reminded her so vividly of his crazed eyes. And Bruno's death had echoed Terror's.

Perhaps the Fear-Dog was not only real but haunting their Pack, seeking revenge for his disciple-dog?

Alpha doesn't believe in the Fear-Dog. She says he isn't real.

But Chase believes. Breeze believes. They thought the Fear-Dog spoke through Terror.

Terror thought that, too.

Storm's head spun, and she stumbled, feeling faint. *How can I fight a Spirit Dog? That is a battle no mortal dog can win.* Despair and fear made her dizzy, and she wanted to howl in misery.

Along her trembling hide, a breeze whispered. Leaves rustled in the branches above her, and the gentle tumbling sound of the river was suddenly clearer. A night bird cried somewhere in the trees, and a beetle scuttled in the grass beneath her paws. It was as if Earth-Dog were trying to wake her up, making the world around her solid and true, a place she could know with her nose and eyes and ears and paws.

No. No, there's no Spirit Dog behind these attacks. That traitor dog is as real as I am.

There was no questioning the facts: Bruno had suffered the same fate as Terror, and that had to mean something. But it did *not* mean that the Pack was being hunted by a ghost. Terror was dead and gone to the Earth-Dog. As for the Fear-Dog: He didn't even exist. Storm knew that in her head and in her heart.

She clenched her jaws and narrowed her eyes. *Think, Storm! Think with your brain, not your frightened belly.*

Bruno hadn't been there on that horrific night. He hadn't been part of that battle. But his death had to point to . . . something. Could the bad dog be one who was there the night of Terror's death?

Many of those dogs had already been targeted by the traitor. Even Whisper, though in that battle he'd fought loyally for Terror.

It wasn't Lucky; she knew that as surely as she knew anything. Lucky would not, *could not* do that to another dog; what was more, he was the Pack's Beta. He had led the Leashed Dogs out of the Empty City to safety, and a new life. And he would never invite fear into the Pack to threaten his own pups. If there was one dog Storm could be sure of, it was Lucky.

Breeze loved the pups, too, and devoted her life to protecting them; Twitch and Moon had both been targets of the bad dog's deadly malice. *Chase?*

Storm pictured the small dog in her mind. She was little, but quick, and ferocious. Chase could stand up for herself; there wasn't much that frightened her, except the imaginary Fear-Dog.

And the bad dog hadn't brought chaos or violence or misery to Chase.

Closing her eyes, Storm tried to go back into her dream. She could recall so vividly the sensations that had flooded her body: fury and infinite strength and a fearless certainty. Nothing had mattered in those moments but putting an end to Terror. She could have torn the jaw off a giantfur, never mind a big, burly, mad dog.

Nothing could have stopped me. Nothing.

Chase was little, but size mattered nothing next to rage. Perhaps Storm wasn't the only dog who had felt that power: the fire in the blood that burned everything it touched.

Could Chase be the bad dog? I know Lucky trusts her, but Lucky trusts every dog.

That's his weakness. . . .

CHAPTER NINE

Dawn was breaking as Storm slipped back into camp, the early rays of the Sun-Dog burnishing the pine trunks and turning the low mist silvery-gold. It was easy enough to sneak past the Patrol Dogs, now that their numbers were stretched so thin. *That should worry me,* thought Storm. *But there's so much more to worry about. And I don't think the biggest danger lies outside the camp.*

How strange it is, she realized as she stepped across the boundary and felt the weight of fear settle once more on her shoulders. *The borders of the camp are what protect us . . . or rather, they are supposed to. Instead, it feels like they're trapping us. We're penned together inside our own territory, like dogs in a Trap House, and danger is right in here with us.*

Still, Storm felt a huge sense of relief as she crept back into her den. She did not want any dog to know she had been wandering alone in the night—not even the ones who were aware of her unnerving problem, like Daisy, Twitch, and Lucky. *Some of my Packmates mistrust me enough already. I can't give them any more reasons to suspect me.*

She felt guilty and ashamed, but she played the part of a dog who had slept the night through in her den, emerging a little while later to stretch and yawn and claw the dewy grass. As it was, she was attracting a few suspicious glances and sidelong stares. Storm ignored them all—she supposed she couldn't blame them for being afraid, even though she *could* blame them for casting their fears onto her.

Her own attention was focused on Chase. The little dog was well aware of her gaze, Storm realized: She kept turning to meet Storm's stare, her own eyes nervous. Her tail twitched and she shook herself uncomfortably as Storm watched her go about her morning duties. *Chase is keeping as much distance as she can between us,* Storm noticed.

I should try not to alert her. But still she couldn't tear her attention away from the small scout dog.

"Storm!" Alpha was padding toward her across the clearing, her ears pricked.

Storm jumped up, glad to have a distraction. "Yes, Alpha?"

"I'm going to send you out hunting with Chase and Thorn, but I want you to combine that with patrolling." The swift-dog swept her tail thoughtfully back and forth. "Because we're so short of Packmates, we are going to have to start doubling up on duties. Just keep an eye on the borders as you hunt."

"Absolutely, Alpha." Storm nodded.

"Wait, Alpha!" Moon was bounding over. "Did I hear you mention Thorn?"

"Yes." Alpha flicked her ears back, surprised. "What's wrong, Moon?"

"I don't think Thorn should be going out just now." Moon's gaze slid toward Storm, and though she quickly looked back toward Alpha, Storm felt a sting of hurt in her chest.

"What, Moon?" she growled. *Is she really afraid that if Thorn goes out in my company, I'll end up hurting her? I thought Moon was on my side—I saved her from that pit! I'd expect this from Snap, but not from Moon. . . .*

Alpha stepped between them before the black-and-white Farm Dog could reply. "There's no reason why Thorn shouldn't go out just now," she told Moon crisply. "Storm, go find her." Alpha paused, then said, "I've chosen Storm to lead this hunt. She is a powerful and *trustworthy* young dog. Do you disagree with my judgment, Moon?" There was a warning in Alpha's eyes.

Moon's ears went back and she shook her head. "Of course not, Alpha. Storm . . . I'm sorry."

Storm nodded, trying not to let her relief show on her face.

"You can tell Beetle at the same time that I want him on High Watch," Alpha added. "Breeze is going there, too. I want dogs to take High Watch in pairs from now on; it's safer."

Chase, ears swiveling toward Alpha, padded up. "You want me on patrol?" she asked. "Did I hear you right, Alpha?"

"A combined hunt and patrol," Alpha corrected her. "We have to use all dogs' talents more flexibly from now on. Go on, Storm. Go and find Thorn."

Moon looked sulky, but she remained silent as Storm and Chase padded off. Storm could feel her haunches prickling with the Farm Dog's glare, but she didn't turn to look back. *I mustn't lose my temper—even though I have good reason to. That would be disastrous right now.*

She slanted a look at Chase, pacing silently at her side. The scout dog was keeping quite a distance from her—a little farther than Storm would be able to lunge, she couldn't help noticing. Tension crackled between them; Storm could feel it in the rising hairs of her hide. She was too angry, though, to break the silence herself. The resentment simmered hot in her throat and chest. *Sending me and Chase out together—this is the worst pairing imaginable right now! Can't Alpha feel it?*

Not a word was spoken between the two dogs as they padded through the trees, so Storm heard Beetle and Thorn before she saw them. Twigs cracked, a body thumped against another body, and there was a protesting yelp.

"Beetle, you have to come at me lower!"

"We're supposed to be practicing for a fight," came his growl. "Block me properly if you don't want to be hurt! I can't help it if your jaw got in the way."

"That's not the point, you idiot. There's no point attacking a tall creature high up! Then they can get at your belly!"

"Not if I'm fast enough." Paws pounded through leaves and there was another thud, and the rustle of forest litter as a dog rolled. "Thorn! That's cheating; stop dodging!"

"*It* would dodge."

"No, it wouldn't, it might have a stick or something. Face me head-on—*I'm* the one who needs to be ready to dodge if it tries to hit me!"

"Fine! Just remember I'm not the enemy. Attack lower down, I tell you. Don't go for my throat first—knock my legs away!"

Storm broke into a bound and pushed through a tangle of shrubs into a small clearing. "Hey, you two. What are you doing?" She tilted her head and frowned as they both turned toward her.

"Practicing our fighting," said Beetle sullenly. His tail was low, and he shot his litter-sister a glance that was half-angry, half-guilty. Thorn nodded, almost imperceptibly, and sat back on her haunches.

"We need to be ready for something like a giantfur," Thorn told Storm defiantly. "Especially if the Pack's moving on somewhere else. We could bump into anything."

Storm narrowed her eyes and looked from Thorn to Beetle. His tail was twitching nervously at the tip, a giveaway sign that he was hiding something. "Giantfurs don't use sticks. And the best tactic for a dog to use on a giantfur is to *run*."

"Well . . . it's like Thorn said," mumbled Beetle, glowering at the ground. "We need to be ready for *anything*."

Chase had followed Storm through the bushes and was looking suspiciously at the two young dogs. "That doesn't sound like any fighting I've ever heard of. You'd be better off practicing moves that'll be useful against a bigger dog. That's what you're more likely to meet, and there are all sorts of tricks you can use. Practice *those*—anything else is a waste of time and energy."

Storm blinked and forced herself not to look at her hunt companion. *Have you been trying out those tricks against a bigger dog lately, Chase?* She gave Thorn and Beetle a low growl. "Anyway, whatever you're doing, it's time to stop. Alpha wants you to come on a hunt with us, Thorn. We'll be patrolling the borders as we go. Beetle, you're to join Breeze up on High Watch."

"Fine." Thorn shook bits of leaf and twig and soil from her fur and trotted forward. "That sounds like a good idea." She hesitated. "Storm, listen . . . can you not mention to any other dog what we were doing? You too, Chase."

Storm flicked an ear forward. "Why not?"

Thorn glanced at Beetle, a look of slight embarrassment on her face. "We want to get it right. It's hopeless trying to practice when lots of dogs are giving you different advice."

Beetle growled in agreement, shooting a meaningful glance at Chase.

"All right," said Storm doubtfully. It seemed a strange request, but Beetle and Thorn were proud and prickly. *I guess they'd hate to make fools of themselves, especially after Chase and I have both told them they're doing it all wrong. Besides, the tension in the camp is still so high, it's probably not a good idea to get any other dog thinking about fighting.* "We won't let on that you're trying out new moves. Not till you're ready."

"Thanks." Thorn wagged her tail and trotted happily to Storm's side. "I'm ready to go. Which direction?"

Storm felt grateful to her. Thorn didn't flinch or avert her eyes or keep her distance; she even licked Storm's muzzle in a friendly gesture.

"Out toward the meadow first, I think, Thorn. We need to more or less circle the camp. Beetle, you'd better head up to High Watch. Breeze must be there already."

"I'm on my way." Beetle turned with a flick of his tail and loped from the clearing.

Thorn stayed companionably close to Storm's flank as the dogs headed toward the meadow, while Chase scampered ahead to scout for prey. With the small dog out of earshot, Storm could forget about her, and she found herself glad, after all, about Alpha's choice of her other hunting partner. Thorn seemed to know instinctively when Storm needed her to head off and circle a likely spot, and she was on constant alert, her nose sniffing the air and the undergrowth, her ears pricked high. Best of all, Thorn was easy company. She didn't fidget and jump all the time, as if expecting Storm to turn and tear out her throat.

I'd almost forgotten how relaxing that is.

Storm was reminded, though, every time Chase doubled back

to make a report. The little dog's head would appear through the bushes, and she'd give Storm a hard and wary glance before telling her where the rabbits were concentrated, or where she'd scented out a likely nest of voles.

She's making me nervous, Storm realized. *Is she watching me like that because she's frightened of me? Or is it for some other reason?*

She might be working out how to catch me unawares. . . .

"There's a big warren up ahead," Chase told them on her third report. "The rabbits are enjoying the sunshine; they don't look alarmed. If we approach from downwind, we can get close enough to catch at least two."

Storm suppressed a shudder. *They're enjoying the sunshine. They don't look alarmed. We can get close enough. . . .*

Is that how you creep up on everything, Chase?

She shook herself. *Don't be ridiculous, Storm—that's how every dog hunts. Don't start feeling sorry for a bunch of rabbits just because she's making you nervous.* "That's good, Chase. Thanks. Thorn, why don't you take the northern flank?"

Thorn tilted her head to one side. "I thought Alpha wanted us not to hunt alone?"

Storm gave a nod. "We're still hunting together. I'll stay low in the grass and go at them head-on from here, and you should be able to intercept them when they run."

"Great, Storm," said Thorn enthusiastically. She spun around and bounded toward the edge of the meadow.

It worked just as Storm had hoped. By the time the rabbits had fled in a panic toward Thorn's ambush, and Storm and Chase had made havoc among the stragglers, they had caught three rabbits between them: two sizable bucks and a smaller doe. Storm stood panting over the corpses, pleased with the result.

"Good work, Thorn. And you, Chase. Right, we'd better not rest on our paws. Let's keep looking." She gave a sharp, low bark as the small dog turned away. "Chase, wait!"

Chase glanced back, one ear pricked, a distinct nervousness in her eyes. The whites showed at their edges. "What?"

She looks like she thinks I'm going to bite her head off. Storm bit back her resentment. "Don't go too far, that's all. Stay in barking distance, and don't go farther than we can smell you. Thorn's right; Alpha doesn't want any of us to go off alone."

"Fine." With a nod, Chase bounded ahead again. Storm flicked an ear toward the undergrowth; yes, she could still hear the rustle of the smaller dog as she moved through the scrub. If there was trouble, she and Thorn could be with Chase in moments.

Thorn trotted at Storm's side once more, calmer now that

she'd used up some energy. "Storm, can I ask you something?" Even for a dog tired from a hunt, Thorn sounded subdued.

Storm twitched her other ear toward her. "Of course. What is it?"

Thorn seemed lost in thought for a few paces, as though arranging her words before she spoke. Pausing, she snuffled at a tree stump, then walked on.

"It's about the day my Father-Dog died. Our Father-Dog."

Storm's heart sank. *I'm not good at this kind of conversation. . . .*

"I've been thinking about it a lot lately," Thorn went on. "Beetle and I—well, we were so young back then. Moon didn't tell us many of the details of what happened to him. I suppose she wanted to spare us."

"I suppose she did," Storm mumbled. Desperately she sniffed the air, almost hoping she'd have to break off this discussion to run to Chase's aid. But the small dog's scent was still clear, and there was no tang of fear or panic in it. *She's fine. And that's good. But quick, Chase, find some prey before I have to answer any awful questions about Fiery. . . .*

Thorn was still talking. "Moon won't talk about that day, but you were *there*, Storm. You sneaked out of camp and followed the search party. You were younger than us, even, but you saw what happened. You had to deal with that knowledge then. So I think we can now."

Storm's heart plummeted even further. "Are you sure?"

Thorn nodded. "I want to know the truth about that day, Storm. Beetle does too. Will you tell us what happened? We want to know how our Father-Dog lost his life."

Storm's pawsteps slowed. This might be awkward and difficult for her, but Thorn had a point. "I think that's fair," she said at last, quietly.

But I'm not sure I want to remember. The details were awful. I'd forgotten how young I was. A shiver ran beneath her fur, for more than one reason. *I wasn't even* Storm *then; I was still* Lick.

But Thorn's right. She and Beetle have a right to know about that day.

She looked into Thorn's eyes—wide, and full of desperate hope—and she knew that she was going to have to walk back into this terrible memory.

"I don't remember all the details," she said at last, truthfully. "But I guess I remember enough. I'll tell you what I can."

"Thank you, Storm," said Thorn. She gave her a sideways glance, her eyes nervous but hopeful.

"It was so unexpected," Storm began. "I remember Fiery got caught in some kind of tangle of ropes. There was nothing he could do—and nothing we could do to help him. Fiery *made* us leave him." In a thornbush beside the two dogs, dew had caught on a spider's web, sparkling and pretty; but the fragile threads trembled from the hopeless struggles of a fly. The spider was already moving deliberately toward its catch. "It was like that," Storm said softly, nodding toward the web. "No dog could help."

Thorn shivered and swallowed. "I remember you coming back to the Food House and telling us. And I remember how our old Alpha said there was nothing we could do, that we had to leave him. Moon was furious."

"I know," Storm sighed. "Remember how determined she was? If no other dog would go after Fiery, she was going to go alone."

"She faced down the old Alpha," said Thorn quietly. "That big, scary half wolf. And Lucky too, and some of the others. I was so proud, and Beetle and I wanted to go with them, but Moon wouldn't let us."

"Lucky wouldn't let me go, either," said Storm with an amused growl. "That's why I had to sneak after them."

"I wish we had, too," muttered Thorn.

"I know," said Storm hesitantly. "But, Thorn? I think it's for the best that you didn't. You can remember your Father-Dog the way you knew him—as a strong and fine and brave dog. He'd only just challenged that Alpha for the Pack leadership, remember."

"Yes." Thorn was quiet for long moments. At last she said, "And when you found him?"

Storm gave a long sigh, closing her eyes briefly. "He was so changed. What the longpaws had done to him . . . I still hate them for it."

"So do I," murmured Thorn. "So do I. But please go on, Storm. Tell me everything."

Storm grunted awkwardly. *This is the most difficult part. I don't know if I can bring myself to say a lot of it.*

"The longpaws had him in a Trap House," she began, and she heard the growl in her own voice. "Well—not a Trap House like the one Alpha talked about earlier. It was more like an enormous loudcage, but the back of it was full of wire traps. And it's just like Alpha described; they were so *small*. No room to run or jump." Storm shuddered. "And your Father-Dog—he wasn't the only one. They had all kinds of animals in there. Foxes, coyotes, birds. There was a sharpclaw, I remember. Even a deer, crammed into such a tiny space. I never thought I'd feel so sorry for prey animals—or for a *coyote*."

Thorn's voice was very small. "What did they do to them?"

"I don't really know, but . . . they gave them bad water, I know that much. It was the longpaws who made your Father-Dog sick. Even after being trapped and stuck behind that wire, he would have stayed strong. But the longpaws poisoned him." Storm's muzzle curled back in a helpless snarl. "They poisoned all those creatures."

"I know," said Thorn. "I've never understood why they'd do that. If they wanted my Father-Dog dead, why didn't they just ki . . . kill him?"

"I never understood why they didn't do that, either." Just the memory of it was bringing all of Storm's fury back. "All of us— Lucky, Bella, Martha, and Twitch, and your Mother-Dog—we got all the traps open. We couldn't leave any creature in that place; it was horrible. A lot of them ran free, but some were too sick to get away. Your Father-Dog was one." Storm swallowed hard. "We managed to get him out of that place, but he was hurt badly."

Thorn was silent, padding beside her.

Storm licked her jaws. "There was a Fierce Dog there. One of the Pack from the Dog-Garden, I think. He was called Axe." She stopped herself suddenly.

Should I even have mentioned Axe? she wondered uneasily. *Do I really want to remind Thorn about our Fierce enemies from the Dog-Garden?*

But Thorn wants the whole truth . . . and it's part of the story. Storm sighed. "Axe was a true follower of Blade, the Fierce Dog Alpha, and I don't think I've ever seen a dog so angry. He hated those longpaws, hated what they'd done to him, and he wanted revenge. We tried to stop him, but he was in such a rage. . . ."

"What happened to him?" Thorn asked breathlessly. "Did he get his revenge?"

"He tried." Storm hunched her shoulders, hating the way she could still see Axe's enraged face in her mind's eye. "He ran straight to their house, a house on wheels, and he challenged them to come out and face him. Well, they did. They came out with a loudstick, and they killed him with it."

Thorn gulped. "They hit him?"

"No, a loudstick's different. The longpaws don't even have to touch you with it. They point it, and it makes a tremendous noise, and a dog drops dead." Storm shook herself. "Don't *ever* go near a longpaw with a loudstick, Thorn. They're deadly."

"But the rest of you, you escaped. . . ."

"We did. We got Fiery away, I guess because the longpaws were busy with Axe. But Fiery was so weak from the poisoned water. When Terror and his crew attacked us on the journey home, he couldn't defend himself. They . . . they killed him, Thorn. He tried to fight, because he was still such a brave, good dog—but Terror's Pack killed him."

"And you killed Terror." Thorn lifted her head, a look of fierce gladness in her eyes. "You protected the Pack, and you avenged my Father-Dog. Terror deserved to die, Storm, and I'm happy you killed him."

Storm said nothing.

Thorn lowered her head again, seeming deep in dark thoughts. Bitterly she growled, "But Terror would never have been able to put a claw on my Father-Dog if the longpaws hadn't done what they did. *They're* the ones who are really to blame."

"Yes," agreed Storm. "But there's no way for any dog to fight the longpaws, Thorn. Axe tried it, and look what happened to him. It was best to just run, and leave them far behind. And to know we should never, ever go near them again."

Thorn padded on for a while in silence. Storm did not feel it was wise to interrupt.

"There must be a way," Thorn muttered at last.

Storm swiveled an ear at her. "What?"

"Nothing."

It wasn't nothing, Storm thought, a chill of trepidation running through her bones. *What did she mean by that?*

But Thorn would not say anything more, and Storm was just

glad the young dog was content with what she'd been able to tell her. Storm hated reliving the past, especially the horrible parts of it, like Fiery's death. Some of the others in the Pack were gentle and empathetic, able to handle such conversations—but Storm wasn't one of them.

Who would have thought just *talking* could be so hard? If only Martha had still been here to explain the horrible events of that day to Beetle and Thorn. *She would've handled it so well,* thought Storm. *Much better than I did.*

It's done now, she decided. *I've told Thorn what I can, and I've warned her about the dangers of the longpaws. Maybe she'll be able find some peace. Just please, Thorn, tell Beetle yourself. Don't ask me to go over it again for him. . . .*

She was just glad down to the tip of her tail that it was all over.

Anxiety was still nibbling at a corner of Storm's mind as the three dogs padded back into camp after sun-high. She shook it off. There were more important things to think about than that awful discussion—real, solid things, like their excellent haul of prey. They'd found another rabbit, out on its own; Thorn had managed to trap a squirrel before it raced up a tree; and Chase had sniffed out a nest—not of voles but of equally delicious rats. *Alpha will be pleased with us,* thought Storm. *And we're all home and safe. Chase couldn't go far from us, but she still found that nest and dug it up. We've done a good job, we kept an eye out for one another, and we're in one piece.*

What was more, they had all remembered to check the borders for strange scents as they hunted, and they'd found nothing untoward. As she and Thorn and Chase passed the boundary into camp, their heads were high, their muscles relaxed, their tails waving loosely. It felt good to be home. One by one they dropped their jawfuls of small bodies on the prey pile, and Storm felt warm with the knowledge of a job well done.

Beetle was already back in camp, his and Breeze's turn at High Watch over for the day. Thorn barked a greeting and bounded over to her litter-brother, and Storm watched them nuzzle and lick each other happily. It was a lovely sight in the late afternoon, but it gave Storm a pang. *I wish at least one of my litter-brothers had lived. I'd have had some dog to talk to, to confide in, to make plans with. . . .*

Sure enough, as she watched, Thorn and Beetle fell into a deep, quiet conversation, their heads close together. Storm sighed, shaking off the twinge of jealousy. Chase had dashed off to be with another group of dogs as soon as the prey was delivered; the scout dog clearly couldn't wait to be out of Storm's company.

"Storm!" Alpha was trotting toward her, her tongue lolling from her slender jaws. "Lucky and I just took a look at the prey pile. What a good catch—well done!"

"The hunt went well." Storm felt a glow of happiness at the praise from her leader. It was quite hard to make Alpha happy these days, with all the stress she was under as both Pack leader and Mother-Dog, and Storm felt as if she'd completed another successful task.

"And you didn't run into any unforeseen problems or dangers?"

Storm shook her head. "Chase didn't scout too far from us, and we all kept each other safe. We each knew where the others were, all the time; the new system worked well, Alpha." She hesitated. *Perhaps now is a good time . . . while the worry is still fresh in my head.* "Alpha, may I speak with you?"

"Always, Storm. I told you that." Alpha licked her muzzle fondly.

Flank-to-flank, the two dogs paced toward Alpha's den, where Lucky, as always, was watching the pups. While they were still out of his earshot—and safely distant from any other dogs— Alpha stopped and turned to Storm.

"I've tried my best, Storm. I've done what I can to stop the other dogs from gossiping about you. I hope—"

"No, Alpha—no, it's not that!" Sitting back on her haunches,

Storm looked steadily at the swift-dog, warmth spreading through her at the thought that Alpha had been standing up for her, even trying to persuade the other dogs she was good. She went on, certain now that she could tell Alpha her worries. "It's not me I want to talk about. It's Thorn."

"Thorn?" Alpha cocked one ear and frowned. "What about her?"

"She kept asking me about Fiery's death. Out on the hunt today. She was desperate to learn exactly what happened."

"Well." Alpha tilted her head thoughtfully. "That must have been hard for you, Storm, and I'm sorry you had to deal with it. But it's natural, I suppose. I'm only surprised she took this long to ask—otherwise I might have been able to deal with it earlier."

"It's not just that." Storm lay down on the ground, sighing and letting her ears droop. "Alpha, she seemed almost too interested. About the longpaws, also. I'm worried she's planning something."

Alpha wrinkled her brow, looking a little surprised. Then she lowered her long body and lay down with her nose nearly touching Storm's. "Storm, listen: I don't want you to worry about this when we have so many other problems. I suspect you're overthinking Thorn's motives. You don't remember your Mother-Dog or your Father-Dog, do you?"

"No, but—"

"Believe me, it's normal that Thorn still talks about Fiery. It's normal that she wants to know as much about him as possible—including his death. It's all part of coming to terms with losing him."

Alpha's dark eyes were gazing intently into hers, sympathetic but a little condescending. Storm could see clearly that the swift-dog did not really grasp what she was being told; she didn't know what it was about the things Thorn had said that had so unnerved Storm.

But I don't know how to explain it. I can barely put it into words in my own head, let alone describe it to Alpha. It was just . . . Thorn's face. Her eyes. Her voice . . .

Briefly Storm shut her eyes, defeated. "All right, Alpha. I understand."

"Good. I'm glad you felt able to come to me, Storm, but on this—I really don't think it's the problem you think it is." Alpha flicked out her tongue and gave Storm's nose a quick lick. "Do you feel better?"

"Yes, Alpha," she lied. "Thank you."

She watched Alpha get to her paws and pad lightly back toward her den. The Sun-Dog was nearly at the end of his run, and dogs were stirring all around the glade, clearly beginning to turn their thoughts toward the prey pile.

I still miss Fiery.

The thought surprised her, and gave her a pang of sadness. The big dog had had such a strong sense of justice and fairness; he might have looked ferocious and brutal, but he had been the gentlest and wisest of dogs. *He was one of the dogs who showed me that a Fierce exterior isn't all there is to me. I learned that just by watching him. And he never acted as if my being a Fierce Dog was anything to fear. If he was still here, would I feel more at home in the Pack?*

Fiery had just challenged the half wolf when he died. That malicious half wolf who so hated Storm and ruled the Pack with cruelty—so many dogs were afraid of going fang-to-fang with him, but not Fiery. Storm's own words to Thorn came back to her. *Your Father-Dog was so strong and fine and brave.*

What would their Pack be like now if Fiery had lived and taken leadership of the Pack? *Would the Pack have broken up the way it did? Or would Fiery have found a way to keep us together?* For a moment she allowed herself to imagine the luxury of a Pack united, a strong Pack, a leader who had identified and dealt with the traitor before that dog could even begin to sabotage their lives. . . .

Storm shook herself. *No. That's disloyal to Alpha. The bad dog is so cunning and deceitful, any leader might have had the same trouble.*

Still, she wondered: Had it all begun when Fiery lost his life? His death had led to Terror's. And Terror's death, she felt increasingly sure, had led directly to all their problems now.

Bruno was killed the same way Terror was. I can't get that out of my mind. It can't be a coincidence.

Storm blinked, her eyes suddenly focusing. Chase was staring straight at her, with an expression of baleful suspicion. Quickly Storm looked away, her gut twisting with alarm.

The Moon-Dog was rising over the treetops, though the sky was not yet dark. *And she is white,* realized Storm. The angry red glow of the previous night had vanished. *Has the Moon-Dog forgiven us?*

Or maybe—just maybe—she's telling me that I'm on the right track. . . . Maybe I'm close to solving the mystery.

CHAPTER TEN

The Moon-Dog was still in the sky when a cold nose shoved Storm, waking her. Disoriented, blinking hard, Storm could make out her pale glow at the mouth of her den. *What? It's still dark. Well, only just . . .*

That wet nose nudged her again, and a voice said, "Storm! Wake up!"

"Lucky?" She staggered to her feet, still bleary from a vague, clinging dream. "What's wrong? What is it?" Shaking her head to clear it, she tensed her muscles and drew back her lip. *If there's trouble, we'll deal with it—*

"Nothing's wrong." Lucky didn't look scared; his tongue was lolling happily.

As her eyes adjusted, Storm could make out figures behind Lucky, all with their ears and tails as high as his. Mickey and Snap stood there—and Chase, she realized with a twinge of apprehension. *This is big for a hunting party these days.*

"We got up to take over the night patrol," said Mickey, gesturing to his mate, "and—well, can you smell it?"

A breath of morning wind stirred the bedding at her paws; Storm flared her nostrils to search it for clues. *Sky-Dogs!* She started. The scent had a sweet-and-spicy edge that was very distinctive.

"The Golden Deer!"

"Yes!" Lucky could barely suppress his excitement. "Will you come with us, Storm? You're one of our best hunters, and I don't want to take any chances."

A thrill of anticipation and pride rushed through Storm's blood. "Of course. Let's go!"

As the other dogs turned to lope away from her den, Storm followed at a run, full of unexpected energy. They picked up speed as soon as they crossed the camp boundary, as if no dog could wait to find the trail.

Two shadows loomed from the trees ahead of them: Thorn and Beetle, returning from their night patrol. They looked surprised, but the hunting party barely paused to greet them, bounding on through the undergrowth. Storm let the joy of running sweep through her, stretching her legs and leaping obstacles with grace-ful ease. As the Sun-Dog's first rays broke through the tree trunks, her nose tingled with the scents of waking prey.

A gray flash caught the corner of her eye, and she veered side-ways in pursuit of a startled squirrel. It fled before her, shooting up a smooth pine trunk just as her teeth snapped on thin air, but she couldn't even be disappointed. She felt happier than she had in days as she doubled back to join the group.

The others looked as if they were enjoying themselves as much as she was. Their tails were high, their tongues lolling, and they barked to one another as they ran, but no dog chatted with Storm.

Lucky was too preoccupied with sniffing the air and peering at the horizon between the trees. *He's been obsessed with catching the Golden Deer for so long,* thought Storm. *Oh, Sky-Dogs, let this hunt be a successful one! If we can catch the Golden Deer, good fortune will come to the Pack. And maybe that good fortune will be followed by more. . . . Maybe the bad dog will be forced out of hiding, and dealt with.*

The Pack could really be happy again. . . .

Snap and Mickey were wrapped up in an intense conversation as they trotted after Lucky, their heads close together and their eyes affectionate. Storm had no intention of interrupting such a private moment. Chase didn't speak to Storm, either, but that was no surprise. The scout dog kept eyeing her—whether with nervousness or malice, Storm couldn't tell—and when Storm caught her gaze, she turned quickly away and ran on even faster.

For an instant Storm stiffened, the glow taken off her happiness; then she forced herself to relax. *Chase acts so anxious around me—if she's really the traitor, and she's onto me, I'll need to act fast. But I'm not sure. I'm going to have to talk to her.*

And that means she'll have to talk to me. . . .

Lucky was slowing down now, and Mickey and Snap were holding back too, all of them sniffing around uncertainly for the Golden Deer's scent. But instead of staying with the hunters, Chase had put on a burst of speed, darting ahead through the bushes to perform her usual scouting duties.

She's not supposed to go so far off on her own . . . Storm thought, and overtook Lucky to follow Chase. The small dog's paws pounded even faster, her legs a blur as she raced to avoid Storm.

What is she doing? Exasperated, Storm speeded up. She bounded after Chase, losing sight of her briefly as she rounded a copse of bushy trees. Storm raced after her, spotting her again, just ahead.

Abruptly Chase skidded to a halt and spun around, sending a flurry of leaves into the air. Her whole body bristled with tension.

"What do you want, Storm?" Chase's glare flicked past

her—checking for the other dogs, Storm thought, but she wouldn't see them, they had fallen behind—and then fixed again on her, full of hostility.

Storm had come to a halt too, blinking in surprise. *She's really scared. I'm scaring her!*

Forcing herself to breathe deeply, Storm took a step back. She lowered her eyes. *Don't look threatening, Storm. That won't help any dog.*

Behind them, she could hear Lucky's trotting paws on the forest floor; Chase seemed to relax a little now that their patrol leader was close by.

Chase's paws shook, but she growled, "Why are you following me?"

"We're on the same hunt." Storm managed to put light humor in her voice. She glanced over her shoulder and saw Lucky, still slowing down and casting about, trying to find the scent again.

Chase wasn't appeased. "You know that's not what I mean."

What now, Storm? Think! "Chase, I . . . I don't know you very well. I was just thinking that last night. We're, ah . . . we're Packmates, and I think we should get to know each other a bit better. Don't you think so?" She licked her chops. "I don't smell the Golden Deer, do you? I think Lucky might have lost the scent. Maybe while he's trying to find it again we could . . . talk."

Oh, Sky-Dogs, that sounded lame. She gazed brightly at Chase, meeting only an apprehensive stare.

"There's nothing to know," snapped Chase at last. She was edging sideways, toward Mickey and Snap, who had entered the broad glade by now.

Storm followed her. "Of course there is," she told her cheerfully. "Where did you live when you were a pup? That sort of thing. Like . . . well, Lucky found me when I was a pup, and he brought me back to this Pack because my Mother-Dog had died. What about you? How did you come to be in Terror's Pack?"

Chase's lip curled up, displaying her white teeth. For a moment, Storm thought she'd blown it. *She won't give me an answer now. Storm, why do you have to be so clumsy when you talk to other dogs?*

Just as she was about to apologize and turn away, Chase snapped, "My Pack left me."

"Oh!" Storm blinked at her. "Oh no. That must have been a bad time for you. Why did they do that?"

"It was the right thing to do," Chase growled. "I was young and sick; what good was I to a Pack?"

Storm thought of Wiggle, her litter-brother. He had been small and sickly, but Lucky would never have abandoned him. . . . "How did you survive?"

"Oh, I'd have starved if it hadn't been for Terror." Chase hunched her shoulders. "He found me, took me in. He gave me a home and Packmates. Terror was a crazy dog," she said, looking defiantly into Storm's eyes, "but he wasn't *all* bad."

Nonplussed, Storm stared after Chase as the little scout dog turned and ran off.

Terror wasn't all bad. . . .

An image of Twitch came to her mind. Their Third Dog had once been a member of the half wolf's Pack; but when he lost all strength in one of his forelegs, the old Alpha threw him out of the Pack, to live or die as chance took him.

But Terror brought him in. Twitch had to chew off his crippled leg while he was in exile, so he only had three to run on—but still Terror made him part of his browbeaten Pack. Terror had bullied and hurt all his Packmates, but they'd stayed, out of fear. Or maybe they'd had nowhere else to go.

Were all of Terror's dogs broken? Storm wondered. *They weren't all starving or crippled like Chase and Twitch, but maybe some of them were broken on the inside.*

Maybe, she mused, they had other reasons for staying.

What would it be like, being a dog like that? Broken and lost, with no Pack to call home?

And how would a dog like that feel when a powerful Alpha rescued them and brought them into his Pack?

I always thought Terror's Pack hated and feared him. Storm swallowed hard. *Maybe I was wrong.*

How might it make such a dog feel, to see her Alpha killed the way Terror was? Maybe Chase resents me because she's angry and grieving. This astonishing new idea rooted Storm to the spot, confused.

She was so preoccupied that she barely heard Lucky's frantic bark. When he repeated it, his voice filled with excitement, she shook herself and turned to stare at him.

"Come on! This way!"

Lucky sprang across the clearing, through a belt of trees, and out into a meadow dotted with cottonwood trees. Caught unawares, Storm had to race to catch up.

Mickey, Snap, and Chase were at Lucky's heels. Storm leaped over a fallen branch and sprinted after them, her confusion forgotten for the moment. *He's scented it! The Golden Deer!*

The small hunting pack plunged into the wood on the far side of the meadow, none of them taking any heed of the racket their paws made on the dry litter left over from last Red Leaf. Storm could smell an elusive, drifting scent, but it was already fading. A good way ahead, there was the crack and rustle of undergrowth as a big animal raced away, fleeter than any dog.

No, this is hopeless, Storm realized with a pang of disappointment. *It's too fast, and it had too big a head start.*

Lucky slid to a halt, panting, but his eyes were shining as Mickey and Snap and Storm trotted to his side.

"That's the closest we've gotten to it yet!" he exclaimed.

Storm watched him fondly. He was almost hopping on the spot in his delight. It was hard to feel too let down when Lucky was so happy just to have come this close.

Mickey shook his head. "You know, I'm not sure that was the Golden Deer," he said. "It might have been just a normal one. I don't think the Golden Deer would make so much noise. It flies like a shadow, doesn't it?"

"It's still a shame we missed it," pointed out Snap, panting. "The Pack could have used a perfectly ordinary deer, too."

Storm flared her nostrils, breathing in deeply, searching the breeze. There wasn't a hint of that spicy, sweet odor; it was hard to tell if the creature they'd chased was the Golden Deer or not.

Still, I'd like to think it was.

Chase caught up to them, her shorter legs trembling as she halted. "No luck, then?"

"No, but we're *definitely* getting closer," said Lucky with satisfaction. "We'll catch that Golden Deer one of these days. It's an omen that we'll get through our troubles." He turned to them with a grin, his tongue hanging from his jaws.

Storm hoped with all her heart that he was right. She wished she could be as optimistic about her strange talk with Chase as Lucky was about not catching the Deer.

Things are more uncertain than ever. If the Wind-Dogs really want to give us a sign, I wish they'd hurry up.

CHAPTER ELEVEN

They had run a long way in their pursuit of the Golden Deer's enticing scent, and the journey back was not nearly so thrilling. Storm's paws dragged on the grass, and her hide prickled with warmth. The Sun-Dog was high overhead by now; she wondered what Alpha would say about their long, unauthorized absence.

Mickey, Snap, and Chase were clearly thinking the same; their tails and ears drooped as they plodded on. Lucky, though, was still in an upbeat mood. It was starting to grate on Storm's nerves.

"Next time we'll catch the Golden Deer. We're getting closer every time, and now we know some of its tricks!" Lucky's tail swished enthusiastically. "If we can just catch it, our fortunes will turn. The Wind-Dogs will reward us by making the new pups wonderful hunters. And if the pups grow up happy and strong, the whole Pack will surely thrive once more!" He bounced along

the path ahead, making Storm want to bite his perky hindquarters. Did he *really* feel as happy as he seemed, or was it all a show,
to keep his Pack's spirits up? If it was the latter, it wasn't working
on Storm. . . .

"Hush, Lucky," said Mickey suddenly, halting.

I'm glad some dog said it, thought Storm, rolling her eyes. But
clearly Mickey had another reason for silencing his leader. He
crept forward past Lucky, placing his paws very quietly.

"We've reached the longpaw settlement," he murmured,
glancing back at the others.

Sure enough, the clearing ahead was a churned-up longpaw
mess. The longpaws must have decided the ruined building a little
way away was beyond repair, so they had started to dig and build
on this open patch of land beside it. The ruin backed onto the forest; the dogs had indeed reached the edge of the town.

Slumbering yellow loudcages rested on the turned black earth,
their great grooved paw marks scarring what had once been grass.
Some of them growled and rumbled softly, and Storm could hear
longpaws barking to one another. Her ears twitched wildly at the
echoes of clattering and clanging.

At least Lucky had stopped chattering and started paying attention. He stood very still, his ears pricked and his nose

sniffing the air. His head swiveled suddenly, and he nodded at a big metal box on the far edge of the clearing.

"Look at that," he murmured. "No—*smell* that!"

Storm sniffed. Sure enough, a scent was drifting powerfully from the box, strong and rich and slightly tinged with rotten things. As the dogs watched from the shadows, a longpaw sauntered up to the box, lifted its top, and tossed something into its gaping mouth.

"Are they feeding it?" Confused, Snap tilted her head to the side.

"Not the box." Lucky grinned mischievously. "Us."

"Huh? But what *is* it?" asked Chase, wide-eyed.

Mickey stood stiffly, watching the longpaw. "It's a spoil-box," he told them. "When a longpaw has something he doesn't want, he puts it in a spoil-box. There's nothing here for us. We should move on." He backed away.

Lucky, though, was quivering with excitement, his tail lashing. "Mickey, you know as well as I do . . ." He licked his jaws. "One of the things they put in spoil-boxes is *food!*"

Storm gaped at him. "Lucky, you're not suggesting we steal longpaw food?"

"Well, *they're* not eating it." Lucky sat back on his haunches.

"Every dog here is hungry, right? We've run a long way and caught nothing."

"But . . . *longpaw* food? Why would any dog want that?" She shuddered.

"I agree," growled Snap.

"Use your nose! Can't you tell how good it is?" Lucky licked at the air itself, drool escaping from his jaws. "We need energy for the return journey, Packmates. And there's food here for the taking."

Eyeing him sidelong, Storm raised her muzzle to sense the odor again. She had to admit that despite the hint of something rotten, it *did* smell good. . . . It was strange, but rich and intriguing.

"But *can* we eat longpaw food?" asked Chase doubtfully.

"Sky-Dogs, yes!" exclaimed Lucky. "It's delicious!"

"I don't know," muttered Storm. "What will Alpha say? What if the longpaws come after us?"

"Alpha won't mind one bit," Lucky reassured her. "As for the longpaws—like Mickey told you, if it's in the spoil-box, that means they don't want it. Besides," he added determinedly, "it'll be good practice for all of us. A dog has to be wily and quick to sneak past longpaws."

"I'm still not sure . . ." murmured Mickey.

"Mickey, *you* know how good it tastes. And besides, we'll still have to go out on a proper hunt when we get back. If we eat a little something now, we'll be better prepared for that, because we'll be stronger. There's no point staggering home hungry, if we're just going to be too weak to catch anything for the Pack." Despite his stern words, Lucky's eyes glinted with anticipation.

"Well, it's true that longpaws are lazy," admitted Mickey. "If they're not in loudcages, they don't chase you far, even if they do see you on their territory. It's just . . ." He half closed his eyes, as if thinking hard. "Well, Lucky, don't you think it's a bit of a Leashed Dog habit, eating longpaw food? I thought we were past that."

Lucky shook his head. "No, Mickey. The longpaws won't be *feeding* us—we're *taking* what we want. From under their noses! It's what I did all the time, when I was a Lone Dog in the city. And no dog ever called *me* a Leashed Dog!"

A small fire of excitement was kindling in Storm's belly, against her better instincts. Lucky made it sound fun. And she *was* rather hungry. And the Pack's Beta seemed to want to cheer them all up. . . .

"I think . . . I think I want to do it," she said slowly.

"Wonderful, Storm! I knew you would." Lucky licked her nose. "Come on, the rest of you—don't lose your nerve. Think of the Pack—and just smell that grease!"

"Fine." Mickey sighed, but his tail too was beginning to twitch with anticipation. "All right, Lucky, you've talked me into it."

"Then I'm in, too," said Snap, with an indulgent sigh.

"And me," added Chase. "I admit, it does smell good."

Lucky's obvious delight made Storm glad she'd agreed to the crazy escapade. He was fizzing with new energy as he led them at a trot around the edge of the churned mud. All of the dogs—except Lucky—cast anxious glances in the direction of the longpaws, but they seemed entirely preoccupied with their loudcages and their tools. There were no loudsticks in sight, to Storm's great relief. As they approached the spoil-box, though, Lucky grew warier, creeping low to the ground and keeping one eye on the longpaws.

The smells from the box were overpowering now, and almost irresistible. Storm felt saliva gathering at the corner of her mouth, and she saw the others licking their lips and jaws.

"Right," said Lucky. "You and I are the biggest, Storm. Let's get into that spoil-box!"

Stretching up on his hind legs, he grabbed the top edge of the box with his forepaws. Storm followed his example, nosing at the lid, and when it came loose at one corner, she seized it in her teeth. It tasted of bitter metal, but she didn't care—the scents coming from inside were just too good.

"That's it, Storm." Lucky worked a paw under the top, prizing it away farther. At last he could shove his whole head in, and suddenly he was scrabbling and kicking, hauling himself up till he was balanced on the edge of the box. Just before he toppled in, he gave a thrust of his shoulders. The lid bounced up and teetered. Taking his lead, Storm took a giant leap, landing on the rim and slamming her forepaws on the lid. It flapped back and fell fully open.

Awkwardly she tumbled down into the spoil-box beside Lucky. He grinned at her. His fur was crusted with crumbs and grease and bits of food, and as she struggled upright she realized, aghast, that her once-shiny coat was the same. Then she caught the scent of the discarded food again, and she no longer cared about the state of her fur.

Both the dogs propped themselves up, placing their paws on the inner rim of the spoil-box and peering down at their companions below.

"We're in!" announced Lucky with a rumble of laughter. "Where are the longpaws?"

Snap wagged her tail. "They're still making so much noise, they haven't heard you."

"Even though you were also making a *lot* of noise," added Mickey with a grin.

"Right. Let's get to work!" Lucky dived back into the spoil-box.

Storm thrust her muzzle deep into the pile of discarded rubbish. "Mmmm!"

"I know!" yelped Lucky. "Look at this stuff!" He grabbed something to show her: a half-chewed meaty bone that was covered in some kind of brown crust.

"Is that *dirty?*" Storm pinned her ears back, but Lucky laughed.

"It's meat—*chicken* is the longpaw word. The brown stuff is something they put all over it, for some reason—well, I know the reason. It tastes *good!*" He threw her the scrap. "Don't eat the bones, they splinter!"

Storm ripped the meat and crust from the bone, chewing. "Oh, it does taste good! Is there more?"

"Plenty." Lucky dug with his paws, tugging out thin boxes with his teeth. He stretched up and dropped them onto the ground outside the spoil-box, where the others were waiting. In a few moments, Storm could hear the rip of paper and the chomping sounds of happy dogs.

Delirious with excitement, she scrabbled in the pile at her paws. A good smell wafted from a bag; she tore it open. Inside were two pieces of soft white stuff with cold spicy meat inside.

"Sandwiches, they call those!" Lucky told her. "And only half eaten!"

Storm was astonished at how good it all tasted. *Why in the name of Earth-Dog would the longpaws throw this stuff away?* She was glad they had, though. Together she and Lucky excavated the pile, eating some of the food themselves, tossing the rest of it out to the others. She couldn't see Mickey, Snap, or Chase, but she could hear their excited yelps, their noisy chewing, and the occasional thump of their paws on the side of the spoil-box as they reached up to beg for more treats.

If this is how Leashed Dogs get to eat, I can almost see the attraction! Storm gulped down a thin piece of salty meat.

"They must be hardworking longpaws." Lucky laughed. "They eat a lot."

"They leave a lot, too," added Storm, licking a wrapper clean of grease. "May the Sky-Dogs look kindly on them!"

Lucky chuckled, raking through paper and boxes and coming up with treasure: a chunk of something that reeked as if it had lain at the bottom of the spoil-box since Ice Wind, but Lucky insisted that was how it was *supposed* to smell. "It's called cheese," he said. "It's delicious."

"I think I'm full," he gasped after he had chomped down half of it. He tossed the rest over the edge to their Packmates with his jaws.

Storm had her snout in a stiff box that held remnants of still-warm, very spicy meat. "There's rice in this," she mumbled through the box. "Like we had in the Food House that time!"

"I don't know if I'll be able to climb back out," groaned Lucky. His belly did look more than comfortably rounded, thought Storm with amusement.

Twisting, she grabbed the edge of the spoil-box with her fore-paws and craned out to look at the others. Mickey was sprawled on his flank, looking content, and Snap had flopped across his legs. Chase was contentedly licking her paws clean of grease.

"I think every dog's full," she told Lucky. "Chase, where are the longpaws?"

The scout dog blinked and twisted her head. Then she gave a yelp of alarm. "There's one coming!"

"Let's get out of here." Lucky hauled himself up onto the edge of the spoil-box and jumped down, and Storm followed him. Both gave grunts of shock as their paws hit the ground heavily. *Oh,* thought Storm, *I've eaten too much.*

Mickey and Snap had sprung to their paws, barking in

warning, and Chase had already begun to run. As Storm and Lucky regained their footing, the four bolted after the little scout dog, as fast as their full bellies would let them.

Storm heard the pounding steps of longpaws behind them; she glanced over her shoulder as she ran. They were yelling, but they were already slowing down. *Just like Mickey said—they're too lazy for a hunt.* One of the longpaws flung an empty box that fell far short of the fleeing dogs, but Storm realized that they were all barking with laughter.

Thanks for the prey, longpaws! she thought mischievously as she raced after her Packmates into the trees.

They couldn't run for long, but they didn't have to. Lucky slowed to a placid trot as soon as the longpaws were out of sight, and the others fell in behind him. Storm licked her jaws. *Oh, I can still taste that crusty bird. . . .*

"I admit it, Lucky," growled Mickey happily. "That was one of your best ideas ever."

"*All* my ideas are the best ever," said Lucky grandly, drawing more amused barks from the others.

Storm picked up her paws happily, a new bounce in her stride. It felt good to have an adventure, she realized—one that wasn't fraught with danger and misery. Her Packmates looked cheerful too, joking and teasing Storm and Lucky about the state of their coats. Once or twice all the dogs paused for a moment so that Mickey, Snap, and Chase could lick the two thieves' greasy fur.

Well, Mickey and Snap had fun licking Storm's fur, nibbling at scraps of food. Chase, she noticed, still didn't come near her. The small dog saved all her joking for Lucky and the others.

Does she know I suspect her? If she is the traitor, does she think I'm onto her? I have to watch her closely from now on.

It was painful to feel so close to an answer, to justice for Bruno and Whisper, and yet still so far away. But perhaps there was another dog she could talk to, if Chase kept avoiding her, one who knew Chase and knew what it was like in Terror's Pack. If Chase was the bad dog, her Packmate Breeze *must* have some inkling of it.

Still, Storm tried to let herself relax and enjoy the attention of the other dogs while she could. She had not felt this lighthearted in a very long time. *It feels good,* she thought. *It feels almost better than "sandwiches" taste!*

By the time they'd gotten closer to the camp, the heavy stuffed feeling had subsided, and they were all ready to go back on the hunt. And with the prey plentiful and their energy fully restored, the five hunters were able to catch several gophers and rabbits for the Pack.

Alpha gave Lucky a rather stern look when the hunters finally padded back into the camp, but between the prey they'd brought back with them, and the fun of the spoil-box story, she didn't stay annoyed for long. The whole Pack hung attentively on their tale of adventure at the prey pile that evening, and the pups especially demanded that the details be told over and over again. Sunshine was thrilled to hear a story that involved nothing more dangerous than some stolen food.

"I wish I'd been there," she confided in Storm as the dogs began to rise and pad to their dens. "It sounded fun!"

"I wish you had, too," Storm told the little Omega fondly, licking her bedraggled ears.

"I want to come next time!" barked Tumble, romping around Storm's paws with his sisters.

Storm laughed. "You're not big enough to climb into the spoil-box!"

"I will be, one day," he said indignantly. "I'm going to be *enormous!*"

"Me too!" yapped Tiny, not to be left out.

"Pups, pups! Leave poor Storm alone!" Breeze trotted up and nuzzled them affectionately. Alpha and Lucky were deep in a serious conversation, Storm noticed; Breeze must have been asked to look after the pups once the Pack had eaten.

"Breeze," Storm greeted her. "I'd like to talk to you, but I guess it's not a good moment?"

"No, it's fine," said Breeze, her eyes bright. "The pups can play a little farther away. Go on, pups, but stay where I can see you!"

"I'll look after them," offered Sunshine. "I'd love to play for a while."

"Oh, Sunshine, thank you," said Breeze warmly.

"Yay!" yelped Nibble. "Yes, Sunshine, come and play!"

With happy yips they tumbled over her, and the little dog led them away to another part of the clearing, chuckling as Fluff and Nibble pounced on her fluffy tail.

The two bigger dogs watched them for a moment, tails thumping the ground in amusement. Then Breeze turned to gaze at Storm.

"What is it, Storm? What did you want to talk about?"

Storm sat back on her haunches and took a deep breath. "I wanted to ask about Terror's Pack. What it was like. You know, life under his leadership . . . was it very hard?"

Breeze lay down, looking thoughtful. "It was certainly difficult. You know how . . . well, the rages he flew into. We had to pad carefully around him."

Storm nodded. "Yes. I can imagine. But do you think any dog misses him? Mourns him, even?"

"Oh, Storm. I don't know. I suppose it's . . . hard to mourn a dog like that. We all lived in fear." Breeze tapped her tail against the ground. "Why are you asking about Terror's Pack now?"

Storm hesitated for a moment. *Can I trust her?*

I have to trust some dog! And Breeze is sweet, and intelligent, and she loves the pups. And she knows Chase, maybe better than any dog. . . .

Tightening her jaw, she made her decision. "It's Chase in particular. She worries me, Breeze."

Breeze tilted her head, studying Storm's face. "Go on."

"I've noticed something." Storm took a heavy breath. "All the dogs who have been targeted, all the victims of the traitor—they were all there the night Terror was killed."

"Are you sure?" Breeze frowned. "Moon, yes. And Twitch . . . but Whisper was a member of Terror's Pack. And Bruno wasn't there."

"That's true," admitted Storm. "But Whisper was there, even though he was on the wrong—I mean, the other side," she corrected herself tactfully. "And Bruno was killed in exactly the way I killed"—she choked slightly on the words—"the way I killed Terror."

"I'm not sure that proves anything," said Breeze doubtfully. "It could be a coincidence."

"Breeze," blurted Storm. "Do you think Chase could be the culprit? The traitor?"

Breeze stared at her for a moment, silent, but her expression was deeply thoughtful. "Storm," she said at last, "Bruno must have been killed by a much bigger dog. Alpha said as much."

"Well, that bothered me," Storm admitted, staring at the ground. "But—oh, I don't know. Bruno was lying there so peacefully—apart from his injury, I mean. Maybe the bad dog caught him when he was asleep? Or maybe his jaw wasn't torn off till he was dead."

"It's possible, I suppose, but . . ."

"You see, I think Chase might have been trying to tell the Pack something," exclaimed Storm. "Sending us a message—showing us why Bruno had to die, why the Pack should be destroyed."

Breeze shook her head slowly. At last she sat up and scratched her ear. Then she reached forward and touched her nose to Storm's.

"No. No, I just can't believe that, Storm. Chase would never do such things. I've known her for a long time and she's a good, loyal dog. A *Pack* Dog."

Storm gazed into Breeze's eyes, worried and suddenly embarrassed. *Have I said the wrong thing? Have I been a fool to accuse Chase?*

"That . . . that does make me feel a bit better, Breeze. If you really think so . . ."

"I do." Breeze nuzzled her gently. "But you've given me a lot to think about, Storm. I won't tell anyone about our conversation, and I'll think hard about this. We have to solve the mystery before anything else happens to the Pack."

"Thank you, Breeze." Storm dipped her head in gratitude and watched the gentle brown dog as she trotted back to the pups.

I'm just glad Breeze didn't bite my nose off for accusing her former Packmate. I'm still not as sure about Chase as she is, but she does have good judgment. And she won't betray my confidence, I'm certain of it.

What made her most grateful of all, though, was that Breeze had taken her seriously. *She was willing to listen. She didn't immediately assume that I must be the one who's responsible. That means a lot.*

Storm padded back to her own den and settled on her bedding. A sense of calm filled her. *I've done what I can for now. And it felt good to talk about it.*

For the first time in a long time, she felt as if she might get a good, peaceful sleep.

CHAPTER TWELVE

When Storm was woken again the next morning, it wasn't by Lucky's gentle prodding her or an excited gathering of hunters. Outside her den there was a flurry of frenzied barks and howling cries. She jerked up, instantly wide awake.

I didn't have nightmares, or walk in my sleep. But these days *any* noise in camp was something to worry about.

She could make out only a few words clearly, but they were enough. *Bad dog. Savage. Breeze.* She shook herself violently and bounded out of her den.

Almost the whole Pack seemed to be assembled, crowding around a figure on the camp boundary. *Not another killing!* Storm's blood froze. She didn't stop running, though. She shouldered through her gabbling, frantic Packmates to the front of the crowd.

Please, not another killing . . .

Breeze was standing there, but she was barely identifiable. Her head and tail hung low, and she was shaking uncontrollably. Her brown hide was covered in bleeding scratches, but the blood was streaky, because she was sodden and dripping and smeared with mud, and there were strands of waterweed caught in her fur. Storm barely recognized her gentle eyes: They were wide and terrified, the whites starkly visible all around them.

"Breeze!" she barked in shock, and sprang forward to press her head to the smaller dog's neck. Breeze flinched as if she was in pain, but she held her ground. Then she sagged against Storm's body for support. Behind her somewhere, Sunshine was whimpering in terror.

"What happened here?" Alpha pushed between Mickey and Chase, looking horrified. "Breeze, what happened to you?"

"I . . . don't know . . . I'm not sure." Breeze couldn't stop trembling. "I woke up being dragged through the woods." She coughed painfully, and a trickle of water ran from her jaws. Her chest heaved.

"By a dog?" demanded Alpha urgently.

"I don't know—yes, yes, I think it was a dog. A big one. I fought, Alpha, I did . . . I tried to howl, but—"

"Hush, Breeze," said Storm urgently. "Save your strength."

"She has to tell us what happened, Storm," said Alpha, a little more gently. "Do you have any idea who it was, Breeze? Did you know this dog?"

"I don't know. I'm sorry, I'm sorry. I couldn't pick out a clear scent over the stink of mud and river-water. And there was also so much of that wild garlic and—so many smells. . . ." She panted, gasping for breath—as much from terror as from exhaustion, Storm guessed. "It pulled me a long way. It was so strong, I couldn't fight it—and then it . . . it flung me in the river. Oh, Storm, the water was so fast and deep. *I thought I was going to drown.*"

"It's all right, Breeze. You're safe." Storm licked at her neck and back, trying to warm her up.

"The River-Dog must have let you go," said Mickey, his eyes wide. "Maybe Martha was looking after you."

"Yes," said Sunshine. "Martha must have helped." She began to whine, mournfully, and Daisy nuzzled her.

"Maybe it *was* Martha," panted Breeze weakly. "Something must have helped me. I managed to swim to shore and drag myself out, but I could feel the River-Dog trying to pull me down." Her shaking grew more violent again, and there was a sob in her voice. "That bad dog was big, Alpha, and it tried to kill me. I know it wanted me dead!"

No dog could say anything. The whole Pack stared at Breeze in pity and horror. Storm could feel the thrill of fear skittering from dog to dog, tingling on every hide.

Twigs cracked as Moon and Snap trotted into camp. The two Patrol Dogs halted and blinked at the gathering of Packmates.

"What happened?" asked Snap as she and Moon exchanged bewildered glances.

"There's been another attack," Alpha told them grimly as they padded over. "You two were on patrol: Did you see anything? Hear or smell something unusual?"

"Nothing," said Moon, gazing at Breeze in dismay. "We didn't smell any intruder. I'm sorry, Alpha."

Alpha curled back her lip, showing her teeth. "Don't feel bad. This traitor is cunning; they masked their scent again. Even Breeze herself couldn't identify her attacker."

"I'm sorry too," said Breeze miserably. Her flanks were still heaving, but she seemed slightly calmer. "If only I hadn't been in such a panic, if I'd focused harder. . . ."

Storm stared at her. *What must that have been like? To be dragged across the ground in darkness by a huge dog—to be so terrified and in pain that you couldn't even recognize your attacker?* Breeze must have been traumatized, Storm realized, and her heart clenched with pity.

"No dog would have been able to think clearly during such a vicious attack," Alpha reassured the gentle brown dog.

"If only I had a *clue*," whined Breeze in frustration, her voice shaking. "I'm furious with myself. I'm so sorry, Alpha. All I know is that it was big. Not Storm, though—it couldn't have been—it was another big dog."

Storm, still propping up Breeze with her flank, tried not to sigh. It was heartening that Breeze still believed in her so strongly that she wanted to get in front of any accusations—Storm was the biggest dog in the pack, now that poor Bruno was gone. But all Breeze had done by insisting how much she trusted Storm was draw every dog's attention. Storm saw a mixture of curiosity and mistrust in her Packmates' gazes.

Sunshine gave a choked howl and backed closer to Lucky. Storm twisted one ear toward her in surprise. *Surely* she's *not scared of me?*

"No dog's accusing any other dog, least of all Storm." Lucky spoke firmly, giving Sunshine a reassuring nuzzle. "The most important thing right now is for us to go out there and try to find some clues while the trail is fresh—if the bad dog has been care-less enough to leave any traces. We have to find this traitor before they strike again."

"We've said that before," growled Snap softly, lashing her tail in frustration. "We've searched and searched, and *still* the bad dog attacks us."

"So now it's more urgent than ever," snapped Alpha. "Lucky's right. We'll go out in teams of three; that seems safest. I will assign each group a patch of territory, and I want you all to search thoroughly. Check every tree stump, every hollow. Look under rocks if you have to; we can't afford to miss anything that might tell us this dog's name."

It didn't take Alpha long to organize the dogs into groups of three; clearly, thought Storm, she wanted to get out there and hunt for clues before the trail could be swept away by rain or wind, or the simple passing of time. Storm herself was teamed with Daisy and Mickey. As soon as Alpha called the names, she felt a rush of relief. There could not be two dogs she trusted more. And at least she hadn't been paired up with Chase again.

This means I won't be able to keep an eye on her. Though . . . I don't think Chase could have dragged Breeze like that. She's too small—this may prove that the bad dog is a large one, or at least a very powerful one. Storm licked her jaws. *But I don't think I could have stood another day working with Chase, anyway. Not when I can smell her suspicion of me.*

The three Packmates set out as quickly as they could, making their way through the forest and across the meadow toward the river. Alpha had told them to check every paw-space of ground between the river and the cave they suspected was a giantfur den, which they always gave a sensibly wide berth—not even a bad traitor dog would risk venturing too close to that.

They moved as quietly as possible, placing their paws with caution on the rustling leaves and grass. Storm's fur prickled with nerves. Fear that she might miss a speck or a hair kept her senses jangling with alertness. *This could be our big chance, after all. There's been no rain since Breeze was attacked. If we can find just a single claw mark . . .*

Even Daisy was quiet and intent, her usual lively chatter silenced. It wasn't until they had paused at the edge of the meadow that she spoke.

"I know it wasn't you, Storm. You would never hurt Breeze."

Storm halted, surprised by the tone of Daisy's voice. There was a hint of desperation in the way she spoke. And the little dog hadn't said, *It's ridiculous!* Or, *Impossible!* Or, *It's out of the question!*

Just: *You would never hurt Breeze.*

And it had sounded almost like she wanted to also ask, *Would you?*

Storm paused, her jaw clenched tight as she waited for the terrible question, but to her relief, Mickey interrupted. "Remember to keep your ears open as well as your nostrils. I don't think we should talk, or distract each other in any way. This is too important."

Storm nodded. *He's right.* She and Daisy once more fell silent, lowering their snouts to breathe in every possible scent as they made their slow and careful way toward the river.

The stench, when it hit her, was sudden and overpowering. And all too familiar—

"Fox!" she snarled.

The others had scented it too: Their heads snapped up at the same moment Storm's did. A reddish-gray tail was just disappearing into the riverside underbrush. Storm bolted after it, plunging into the bushes, her whole head filled with the fox's musky odor.

The fox was quick and nimble, darting between rocks and squirming under thornbushes that Storm couldn't hope to penetrate; but she could hear Daisy scrambling through the brush, coming after their quarry at a wide angle. She was aware, too, of Mickey's running paws on the edge of the meadow, skirting the bushes but keeping pace with the sly creature. *All I have to do is keep harrying it,* she thought grimly. *However fast it can wriggle through brush, Mickey's going to overtake it once we're on the flat land.*

Sure enough, as she raced up a low slope through a tangle

of branches, she saw Mickey's shape up ahead; he was facing her and the fox, his shoulders low and hackles high. His bared teeth glinted in the light. From the side, she saw Daisy tearing through the scrubby undergrowth, dodging obstacles with agile grace despite her stubby legs.

The fox scrabbled to a halt when it saw Mickey, and Daisy was blocking its escape toward the meadow. With a squeal of fear, it spun and hurtled back the way it had come.

Storm was ready for it. She braced herself on her forepaws, lunging forward and snarling. The fox, out of options, tried to skid to a stop and tumbled head over heels. Sprawling in front of her, it rolled swiftly onto its belly and cowered.

"Dogs not hurt fox," it rasped, its tongue hanging out of its jaws. Its eyes were angry and scared.

"That depends on you," growled Storm.

Abruptly the fox's eyes popped wide, and recognition sparked in them. "Ah! Ah! Good dogs, yes, you dogs not hurt poor fox."

"What?" A sickening claw of dread tugged at Storm's gut. *Wait a moment—this fox looks familiar—*

"You good dog. Well. You not-so-bad dog. You let poor fox go now. Yes, yes. Let fox go."

Daisy and Mickey were behind the creature now, blocking its

escape, and they were both staring at it—Mickey with guilt in his eyes. The fox glanced over her shoulder.

"You not-so-bad dog too." She sat up on her haunches, looking more confident. Ignoring Daisy, she stared straight at Mickey. "You smart dog like this one. Yes, two of youse. You let Fox Mist go now."

Storm shot Daisy a nervous glance. The little dog was watching the fox, appalled. Hesitantly Daisy stepped closer, sniffing; then she flinched back in revulsion at the strength of the odor. She walked a full circle around the creature, studying her from ears to paw-tips.

Daisy's dark eyes turned to Storm, then to Mickey.

"Isn't this the fox we captured before?" she demanded. "This is the one Alpha told us to punish."

"Um, it could be . . ." began Storm.

"I'm . . . not sure I would recognize . . ." Mickey licked his chops.

"Yes, yes!" interrupted the fox. Storm saw Mickey wince. "That Fox Mist! Now you let go again."

"What?" Anger flared in Daisy's eyes. "You two were supposed to mark her. She looks pretty unscarred to *me!*"

Fox Mist was creeping delicately toward the gap between

Storm and Daisy. Storm slapped a paw on the ground to stop her. "Just stop right there," she growled.

The fox flinched and sat down again, curling her tail around her rump and placing her head on her forepaws as if she wanted to look as small as possible. Storm couldn't stomach the idea of hurting her, though. Her sly little escape attempt had at least given Storm a chance to avoid Daisy's angry question.

Storm lowered her head to glare straight at the fox's nervous face. "You've obviously been slinking around our territory all night. Did you see anything?"

"What anything?" The fox seemed to decide on a change of tactics, tilting her head winsomely. "What means nice dog, good dog?"

"Stop that stupid flattery." Storm growled low in her throat. "Anything odd. Strange dogs prowling. Unusual behavior. You're not a fool—you know the kind of thing I mean."

"I see not anything." The fox hunched her shoulders in a gesture of helpless apology. "Nothing funny, no dogs I don't know. Only dogs from nice dog's Pack, they sniff the ground, they look everywhere, foxes go hide."

"That would be Moon and Snap on patrol," growled Mickey. "That's no help."

The little fox shrugged again, her eyes open and innocent. "All dogs is looking the same to me anyway." Suddenly she brightened. "No, I see something!"

"What?" Storm tensed. "What did you see?"

"I see dead dog." The fox frowned solemnly. "Dog all dead, dog all bitten and dead. Just like poor fox cub in forest." For an instant, her expression hardened and grew viciously hostile; then she seemed to master herself, and the submissive tone was back. "Up on cliff. Poor, poor dog."

"That was days ago." Storm's belly clenched in disappointment.

"Yes, yes. Two fox-moons, three fox-moons, maybe. Big, big dead dog. I see big dog get dead."

Storm started. "Wait. You *saw* Bruno being killed?" Her heartbeat raced, thrumming in her throat and chest. *This is it! She saw the murderer!*

Mickey's and Daisy's jaws had fallen wide, and they exchanged shocked glances. Daisy jumped to her paws; her eyes slanted, a little guiltily, toward Storm, before fixing excitedly on the fox. "Was it a dog you'd seen before? A dog you *knew*?"

The fox lifted a paw to lick it, looking smugly pleased at their reaction. "I not know dog."

Daisy's little body sagged with what looked, to Storm, suspiciously like relief. "Another big dog, then?"

Storm stared. *What do you mean, 'another big dog'?* Sadness threatened to choke her. *Oh, Daisy, you honestly thought the fox was going to name me, didn't you?*

"'Big' dog?" The fox set her paw back down. "How I know?" she scoffed. "I tell you, all dogs is looking same! Fox little!"

"But you must have *some* idea!" cried Daisy. "Look at me, look at Mickey here, look at Storm. You must have been able to tell what sort of size the killer was!"

The fox narrowed her eyes, tilting her head to one side and studying all three dogs. "Humph," she said at last. "This dog that kill dogs *and not just fox cubs*—it not so big. No, not so very, very big. Maybe not bigger than *you*."

She was looking straight at Daisy.

Mickey looked as stunned as Storm felt. Daisy was just blinking, speechless.

"How can . . . ? That's not possible!" yelped the little dog.

"It's not," barked Mickey. "A dog Bruno's size, taken out by a dog your size? It's *not* possible. It's ridiculous!"

Except that I thought not so long ago that it was perfectly possible, remembered Storm, *if Bruno's jaw had been gnawed off* after *he was killed.* But still . . . it did not seem likely. *A dog of Daisy's size would have exhausted itself biting off Bruno's jaw. . . .*

The three dogs were so taken aback, they were too slow to react as the fox shot suddenly past Storm. A streak of gray, she vanished into the bushes with an impudent flick of her tail.

"Let her go," growled Mickey angrily. "She's clearly told us all she knows."

"Sure," said Daisy, her voice brimming with fury. "Let her go—just like *you* two did before!"

Storm licked her jaws, distressed. "Look, at least now we know something—"

"*How* can either of you believe a word a fox says?" demanded Daisy. "You can't trust a fox! And you can't make *friends* with them!" The little dog's hackles bristled; her legs were stiff and her tail quivered as she glared at Storm and Mickey. "How could you have let her go? You said you'd punished that fox! You *lied!* You lied to our Alpha!"

"Daisy," pleaded Mickey, "you have to understand. We're not *friends* with that creature, we just—it seemed wrong to scar her. It would have been . . ."

"Unnecessary," put in Storm.

"Yes, and *brutal*," Mickey added. "She was pregnant with cubs!

We thought it would be wrong."

"What does it matter what you thought?" Daisy looked less furious now, and more stunned with disbelief. "That wasn't your decision to make—you had no right to judge! You went against Alpha's orders, both of you!"

"We . . . we just couldn't go through with it," began Mickey, but Daisy gave an angry yelp, cutting him off.

"And *then* you came back to camp and you *lied!*" Her dark eyes blazed. "You lied in our faces. You lied to the whole Pack."

Storm couldn't say a word. She was too shocked by the sight of Daisy in a rage—*a justifiable rage,* she realized miserably. The little dog's face was full of horror, and revulsion, and worst of all, savage disappointment.

"You lied to us all," Daisy spat, turning her tail on both of them. "How can any dog trust either of you now?"

CHAPTER THIRTEEN

"I cannot believe this. I can't. But I have to."

Alpha's voice was like a longpaw whip, cutting Storm to the bone. She had no idea what her leader's expression was like; she couldn't look at the swift-dog's face. Storm just stared at the ground beneath her nose, wishing she could sink into it and hide between the Earth-Dog's paws for a while: maybe a whole turn of the Moon-Dog. It should be easy enough: Like Mickey beside her, she was already pressed low to the ground, submissive and ashamed.

Alpha's terrifying, enraged voice rose to a howl. "The pair of you betrayed the Pack!"

"We're so sorry, Alpha," whined Mickey.

"You!" Alpha snarled at him. "I would never have believed this of *you*, Mickey!"

Against all her better instincts, Storm's hackles began to rise. *What does Alpha mean by that? Is she saying that she* would *expect it from me?*

Remorseful as she was, it burned Storm's pride that she had to cower here in front of Alpha with the whole Pack watching. *I don't care what they think. It* would *have been wrong to wound that fox for no reason. It was a stupid order!*

I know we shouldn't have lied to the Pack. But I'm not sorry I took mercy on that fox. I'm not!

Resentment burned in her belly, a small ember of pure rage and hate. Didn't they all call her dangerous? Didn't they think *she* was the brute around here?

Yet their beautiful swift-dog Alpha was the one who'd given that stupid, brutal command—*and she stands there implying that she wouldn't have expected better of* me!

And humiliating me like this, in front of the Pack that already distrusts me . . .

Aware that her bitter fury must be showing in her eyes, Storm forced it down like a tough bite of prey. *I have to submit. It's Pack rules.*

Just bear it, Storm.

Still unable to look at Alpha's face, she flicked a quick glance at the rest of the Pack. None of them looked sorry for her, or even for Mickey. Every dog avoided her eyes, but she could see that their expressions were sullen and angry.

"Disobeying an order's bad enough," barked Chase, "but lying to the Pack?"

"It's not acceptable. I don't care if they thought they knew better than Alpha." That was Daisy, still clearly seething with shock.

"No dog knows better than their Alpha," came Sunshine's small voice. "That's Pack law."

Sunshine? The little Omega's disapproval hurt Storm worse than any other dog's contempt.

"You will both eat last tonight." Alpha's tail lashed the air. "And not just tonight. That will only be part of your punishment; you both need to learn a harsh lesson."

"Alpha." Storm lifted her head defiantly. "If the fox had been terrified of us, it wouldn't have talked to us. At least we know now that Bruno's killer was a smaller dog."

"Hah!" barked Moon with contempt. *One of her pups was killed by a fox,* remembered Storm. "You believe a single word a fox says? Are you really that foolish, Storm?"

Lucky was gazing at Storm with pained disapproval. "That fox wanted to get away from you—it would have said *anything*, Storm. Foxes cannot be trusted. Not ever."

"But, Lucky—"

"And what's more," he growled loudly over her protests. He glared at her. "What's more, foxes are cunning. It would take one look at you and know what you wanted to hear: that the killer was a small dog, smaller than *you*."

Storm felt as if he'd kicked her in the ribs with his hindpaws. "Lucky, that's not true, you know it's not. There were three of us there and—"

"That's enough!" He silenced her with a cold bark. "Be quiet, Storm. You've said *more* than enough. Don't talk to me again until you're ready to be a true Pack Dog."

She couldn't speak. She stared at him, the hurt burning through her like a forest fire. She could only plead with her eyes— *Lucky! You know me better than this. . . . Or, are you the same as the others? Have even you always been suspicious of me, deep down?*

Lucky stared at her for a few long moments, then turned away in disgust.

The mood among the Pack was dark as they gathered around the prey pile later that evening. Storm found it hard to care that she and Mickey would be the last ones to eat; misery and anger had killed her appetite anyway.

There was none of the chat and banter and joking that usually accompanied the assembly of the Pack. Subdued, arriving in ones and twos, every dog lay down, heads on their paws, and watched the prey pile silently. Alpha sat in her usual place, her face stony. Lucky, beside her, was solemn and thoughtful; even the four pups were quiet.

What Mickey and I did seems to have been the last bone that choked the dog. I'm sure in normal times, Alpha wouldn't be this angry and unforgiving.

It was as if Alpha's and Beta's approval and trust had been a strong beam of sunlight warming her flank, and now the Sun Dog had hidden behind a black cloud, and she felt even colder than before he'd turned his face on her.

One by one, Alpha called up the dogs, her voice short and sharp. Any low conversations that accompanied the Pack's meal were stilted, and soon over. No dog seemed especially hungry. Storm thought with longing of how she and Lucky had raided the longpaws' spoil-box with Mickey, Chase, and Snap. They'd had so much fun, and they'd joked and boasted with the Pack about their escapade. Every dog had liked them, and every dog had appreciated the prey they'd brought back.

How can things have changed so quickly?

At last Omega had eaten her fill, and Alpha barked, "Mickey."

179

As the Farm Dog sloped forward, his tail low, Storm thought, *Even Mickey gets to eat before me. It's obvious who Alpha blames most.*

When it was her own turn, Storm grabbed a rabbit leg and returned sullenly to her own place, gnawing at it with little interest. She was still eating when Alpha growled, "Pack, I want to hear your reports. What did the patrols find today?"

"Not much," said Moon wearily. "We saw some blood, on the path and on bushes. It was Breeze's." She nodded at the brown dog, who still looked weary and nervous. "There were tracks in the path, like something had been dragged along—but we couldn't make out any other scent."

"It was the same with our area," added Snap. "We saw the trail, but caught no scent. This dog is cunning."

"We didn't see anything," said Thorn apologetically. "But then, we weren't where Breeze said she was dragged. We tried to find any spots the bad dog might have crossed as it approached the camp, but there was nothing. Not a single paw mark."

"Whatever dog we're up against, it's horribly clever," said Sunshine in a small voice.

"Yes," agreed Alpha. "You haven't remembered anything else, Breeze? Anything that could help us?"

"I'm sorry." Breeze's head and tail drooped. Her scratches had stopped bleeding, but they still looked nasty. "It was so confusing. And terrifying. And so dark."

"It's all right," said Alpha, though she growled the words through gritted teeth. "It's not your fault." As she said that, she turned her head to gaze directly at Storm and Mickey.

As if it's our fault! Storm felt hot rage in her throat.

"Storm. Mickey." Their leader's voice was curt. "You will take High Watch tonight."

"Yes, Alpha." Mickey crouched submissively, his tail tucked between his legs. That was probably more sensible, Storm thought, than glaring in defiance. But she couldn't help it.

"Not just for tonight," Alpha went on. "You will both stay up there for three full journeys of the Moon-Dog and the Sun-Dog. You can take turns sleeping, to relieve each other during no-sun."

Storm got to her paws, shaking at the injustice, but she couldn't speak—even if Alpha would have allowed her to. Instead, the swift-dog went on, "Your time on High Watch would be longer, by the way, if the Pack didn't need you to hunt. And when you return? You will both still be held in disgrace. You will be considered bad dogs until you prove yourselves worthy of the name Pack Dog once more."

The rest of the Pack remained motionless, staring at Storm

and Mickey, but Snap bounded to her paws. "Alpha!"

Alpha didn't even look at her. "Yes, Snap?"

Storm saw the way that Snap's tail was quivering and knew what the small dog was going to say. *I don't even have the energy to growl at her now. . . .*

"That's where Bruno was murdered! You can't send Mickey up there for three days—not with *Storm!*"

"Quiet," said Lucky tersely, standing up. "That's enough, Snap. This is Alpha's decision. Mickey will be fine."

"You don't know that—!"

"Beta said *enough!*" Alpha turned at last to Snap, glowering. "If Mickey and Storm trust each other enough to conspire against the Pack, and defy my orders, then they can certainly trust each other on High Watch."

There was no sound for a moment. Snap stepped back, still looking unhappy.

"Now," said Alpha. "Both of you. Get yourselves to High Watch, and out of my sight."

CHAPTER FOURTEEN

Distantly, from across the river and the meadow, the noise and clatter of the longpaw town was winding down. Some lights flickered off; others began to shine like tiny Moon-Dogs as the gray dusk deepened. Longpaws barked farewells. Loudcages growled, rumbled away, and faded.

It was funny how far sounds traveled, thought Storm, gazing down toward the broken settlement. *The place is just as far away as it was before, but the noise is so much clearer from up here. The Wind-Dogs must carry it.*

Behind her, Mickey paced up and down the path the Pack had beaten on the cliff top. He looked so tired, Storm realized, but he was trying to keep himself alert. He kept turning, almost against his will, to look at the rock where Bruno's body had been found.

With weary paws, his head sagging, he plodded over to where

Storm sat looking landward. "Have you seen anything new?"

"No," she sighed. "It's just the same as last night."

"I'm starting to wish that something *would* happen," yawned Mickey. "It would be less tiring if we had something to do."

And we'd be of much more use to the Pack, thought Storm resentfully. *I don't think I can stand another day and night of this. Another idiotic decision from Alpha, though I'd better not say so to Mickey.* "I don't want to be assigned to High Watch again till next Tree Flower," she grumbled. "I'm sick of this."

Mickey made a sound that might actually have been agreement; Storm wondered if he was as annoyed at Alpha as she was. "Well, it'll be over soon."

"Yes, though not soon en— Wait, what's that sound?" Storm got to her paws and pricked her ears, staring down at the longpaw town. "Look. It's Beetle and Thorn! What are they doing?"

Mickey came to her side and peered down. The dusk was deepening, but the weak glow that lit up the digging-and-building area picked out the movement at the fence quite clearly. Yes, it was Moon's two pups. Thorn had already scrambled beneath the high wire fence; behind her Storm could make out Beetle, clawing at the ground, flattening his back to wriggle through and join his litter-sister. Both the young dogs stood for a moment, scratching and shaking themselves, and peering around the raw earth and new walls.

"What in the name of the Earth-Dog are they up to?" Mickey blinked and tilted his head.

"I don't know." Storm licked her jaws. "Looking for food?"

"In there? I doubt it."

So did Storm, to be truthful. "Maybe Alpha has sent them on a scouting mission?"

"I doubt that, too." Mickey frowned. "Alpha wants us to keep as far away from the longpaws as possible, doesn't she? I don't think she'd send Thorn and Beetle on such a dangerous mission. It's not as if they're familiar with longpaws and their ways."

Storm shifted, sat down, and scratched her ear. "If they're doing this without permission, and Alpha finds out, she's going to be in an even worse mood."

Mickey shot her a half-amused glance. "Well, we're the ones who put her in the bad mood to start with. But we should tell her what they're up to." Morosely he added, "Maybe she'll still be so mad at us, she'll go easier on Thorn and Beetle."

Storm licked her jaws. "Or they might end up on punishment duties too. And it's not like the Pack can afford that. It's enough of a waste leaving the two of us up here licking our paws." There was something else, too—she'd had a perfectly good reason for breaking the Pack's rules, and as much as she regretted the lie, she didn't regret letting Fox Mist go, not one bit. What if Thorn and Beetle had a good reason too? How would they feel about the dog who reported them to Alpha?

Thorn and Beetle seemed to like Storm, to believe that she was innocent. If they were caught and punished because of her, when they weren't doing anything *bad*, would they ever forgive her?

Mickey's brow furrowed; he seemed to be thinking deeply. "Well . . . perhaps we shouldn't tell Alpha right now, then—but we should mention it to Moon in the morning. I'm sure she'd want to know."

Storm squinted to stare down at the longpaw settlement. She could just make out Thorn and Beetle, now creeping in and out of the shadows, sniffing at sleeping loudcages, standing up on their hindpaws to investigate what lay behind the new walls. Thorn gestured with her head to Beetle, and the two litter-siblings vanished around a corner.

"I know what it's like to have dogs watching you, talking about your mistakes," Storm told Mickey. "Thorn and Beetle are grown dogs, with their own Pack names. We shouldn't be reporting back to Alpha, or their Mother-Dog, on what they're up to. In fact, telling Moon might be even worse. It doesn't look like they're working against the Pack, and I don't believe they ever would."

Mickey sighed. "I don't know, Storm. We're supposed to be watching for unusual activity, and that's *very* unusual activity. And the idea of keeping anything from Alpha, now of all times—"

"Mickey, listen," said Storm, remembering what Alpha had told her before, in a friendlier moment. "Thorn and Beetle—well, they've been struggling with the way Fiery died. And they're a bit obsessed with longpaws. So maybe sneaking off to that place is just their way of finding out more about them. It's natural, don't you think?"

"I suppose so." Mickey's eyes softened. "We all miss Fiery, so I can imagine how hard it is for those two. Fine, Storm: I won't mention it to Alpha. Or to Moon."

"Thanks, Mickey. I really do think that's wise."

"But," he added sternly, "I'm going to have a talk with Beetle and Thorn tomorrow. Longpaw settlements are dangerous. I know better than any dog that some longpaws have good intentions—but a lot of them don't." He shuddered. "And even the places where they live and work can have hidden dangers. Loud-cages, machinery—I'm going to have to impress on those two what a risk they're taking."

Storm nodded. "That's fair, Mickey."

He licked her ear. "I'm going to go and see if there are any floatcages around." He turned away and padded over to the edge of the cliff, then sat down, curled his tail around him, and gazed out across the Endless Lake. Storm wondered if she too should watch for the giant floating vessels that carried longpaws on the water, but her time would be better spent, she supposed, keeping an eye out in the other direction.

At the edge of her vision was the huge boulder that had concealed Bruno's body. She couldn't help her gaze slanting toward it. In her mind's eye, she relived the scene again: the brutal injury, Bruno's body covered in so much blood. *Could a small dog really have done that to him? Was I crazy to think it could have been Chase?*

The fox said the killer might be no bigger than Daisy. But that creature admitted herself that she isn't good at judging a dog's size or appearance. "The same size as Daisy" could mean any dog from Sunshine to Mickey, for all Storm knew. *And that's if she is even telling the truth.*

There was a sudden scratch of claws on dry rock, and Storm jumped, her heart thrashing. But the dog who came into view at the top of the steep cliff path was only little Sunshine, followed by Moon. Moon was still limping slightly, Storm noticed; the

Farm Dog was using her wounded paw with great caution. Storm was glad they had decided not to mention Thorn's and Beetle's movements—if Moon knew they'd sneaked off, she would only go rushing after them, and her paw was still weak and sore from her fall.

"How is that paw doing?" Mickey, walking over, cocked a concerned ear at Moon.

"It's a little better, thank you. Still sore, though." Moon licked at it, looking faintly annoyed.

"And how are things in camp?" Mickey went on, a look of longing in his eyes.

"It's all right," Sunshine told him. "Quite quiet, really. Oh! I have to tell you what happened with the pups. Yesterday, they asked the Patrol Dogs to bring back any feathers they found, and no dog knew why. They were in their den for ages and ages this morning, and every dog thought they must be taking a nap." She gave a high yelp of laughter. "We should have known better! When the pups came out, they'd stuck the feathers into Fluff's fur, all over—because she'd decided she wanted to be a Sky-Dog! Beta had to tell her the feathers wouldn't make her fly, and she was *so* disappointed—but oh, Sky-Dogs, it was funny." Sunshine's tongue lolled. "It took Breeze forever to get the feathers out, but when she was finished, Lucky gave Fluff a ride around the glade on his back, to make her feel as if she was flying. And then of course all the pups wanted a turn—" Sunshine ran out of breath, and at the same time seemed to register Storm's and Mickey's bleak stares. "Well, anyway, that kept the pups busy for a while," she finished lamely.

I never thought I'd feel so miserable about missing an ordinary day in camp, Storm thought. *I wish I'd seen that, even if it was only silly pup antics.*

She had a suspicion Mickey felt the same way. He cleared his throat. "That sounds fun, Sunshine. And, Moon, how are Beetle and Thorn doing?"

Storm shot him a warning glance, but Moon didn't seem to pick up on the edge in Mickey's voice. "They've been volunteering for a lot of patrols," she told them. "I worry that they aren't getting enough rest, but I have to admit, it's been helpful. The Pack has needed all paws working, especially in the last few days. . . ." She licked her jaws, seeming to realize her words were a little tactless.

But Storm wasn't worried about that. *It was Alpha's decision to send two of us into exile up here; I'm not going to feel guilty that the Pack is shortpawed.*

What worried her more was Thorn and Beetle, and their nighttime expeditions. *That must be how they've been sneaking out:*

pretending that they're on a legitimate patrol.

A shiver of anxiety rippled through her fur. *If Moon had any idea that they're not patrolling at all, she would run right off High Watch and go running after them—and that's the last thing she, or the Pack, needs right now.*

Those two had better prove me right. . . .

Storm had the distinct feeling that Alpha regretted putting two of her most capable Pack members out of action—not that she'd ever admit it. The swift-dog sat on her haunches, giving Storm and Mickey her most severe gaze, tapping her tail briskly against the ground. Her eyes were tired and her fur looked dull. *Well,* thought Storm, *every dog must have had extra duties for the last three nights and days and I guess that included Alpha herself.*

"You may have finished your sentence at High Watch," Alpha told them, "but that does not mean you're forgiven, either of you. You are back among the Pack because we need you as hunt-dogs."

"Of course, Alpha." Mickey nodded, subdued.

Storm said nothing. The Moon-Dog, half turned away, was already high in the dark-blue sky; prey-sharing had been over by the time she and Mickey descended wearily from High Watch. At least they would get a night's sleep in their comfortable dens, but they wouldn't get a proper meal till the following evening. After the last few days of scant pickings on High Watch, that seemed harsh to Storm.

"You'll continue to eat last when we share the prey," added Alpha, as if she were digging in a claw. "That is, until you each prove to me that you're capable of being true Pack Dogs again. I hope you realize how disappointed I remain in you both."

That's been made more than clear, thought Storm bitterly as she and Mickey turned to plod toward their dens. *I wish I could feel more penitent about what we did. I know it was wrong.*

But Alpha is making it hard to be sorry.

Mickey didn't seem to feel the same way; he looked genuinely remorseful as he padded at Storm's side, his ears low and his tail tucked between his legs. But he lifted his head with sudden curiosity as Beetle and Thorn trotted past them, heading for the woods.

"There they go on patrol again," he said softly. "Or maybe not."

He and Storm exchanged a look of misgiving.

"There's nothing we can do," she told him with a hunch of her shoulders. "I really don't think it's wise to interfere. They're both smart enough to stay safe."

Mickey nodded doubtfully and turned toward his own den. *He's still planning to give them a lecture when he gets the chance,* realized

Storm. *That's fine by me. They deserve it.*

But I think they'll be all right for now. What I told Mickey is true: Fiery's pups aren't stupid.

With a sigh she squeezed into her den and trod a circle on her sleeping-place. The camp was quiet, but after the long time with only Mickey for company, it was reassuring to hear the sounds of other dogs, shifting and scratching and occasionally growling in their sleep. From a little way away, she could even hear Lucky's distinctive snoring. It was a combination of deep snorts and high squeaks that she'd always found secretly funny, but for the moment, she'd lost her sense of humor. Storm glowered at the den walls.

One of her ears pricked up. There was another sound now, one that didn't come from a sleeping dog. She could hear cautious steps; they sounded hesitant, and the dog was placing its paws as lightly as it could on the grass. Storm's brow furrowed. She raised herself up on her forepaws and cocked her head.

That's not a dog going out to make dirt. That's a dog who does not want to be heard.

Standing up, Storm pushed her head out of the den opening. It took only moments for her eyes to adjust, and she was in time to see a familiar rump and tail vanish into the trees.

Chase!

All her suspicions, all her fears came flooding back. *Where is Chase going at this time of night? She can't be up to anything good—not sneaking around like that.*

It certainly wasn't something Storm could ignore. Quietly she emerged from her den and slunk after Chase, trying not to disturb any other dog. *Whatever it is, I can deal with it myself. And with my reputation the way it is at the moment, I'm going to need hard proof before I accuse her of being up to something.*

Chase's scent was clear on the night air, and it didn't take Storm long to catch sight of her. Just as she'd suspected, the little dog didn't go only far enough to make dirt; she was pressing on through the undergrowth, leaving the camp boundary far behind her. Determined not to alert Chase till she'd found out what she was up to, Storm followed as closely as she dared.

Clouds scudded across the half-obscured Moon-Dog, and there were few stars; Storm had to focus hard to keep Chase in view. She had expected the little dog to stop beyond the boundary of the Pack's territory, but still she trotted on, giving an occasional nervous glance to her side or over her shoulder. *She looks shifty,* Storm decided. *What will I do if I catch her in the act of some bad deed? Will I have time to go back to alert the Pack, or should I deal with it myself?*

Will the Pack even believe me?

She picked up her pace, exasperated and increasingly worried.

In the name of the Forest-Dog, how far is Chase planning to go?

Just as she thought it, her question was answered. Ahead of Chase, a second shadow appeared through the trees: a scruffy-looking dog of around the same size, who bounded up to her with friendly woofs.

The shattering of the nervous silence took Storm by surprise, and she came to an abrupt halt, blinking. More dogs were emerging from the shadows now, and they looked familiar. Crouching low, Storm slunk closer.

Their smells . . . I know these dogs!

Now she could see and smell them all clearly. That dog who was nuzzling Chase was Rake, her old friend from Terror's Pack. The scruffy dog's companions were familiar, too: Storm recognized Woody and Ruff—and there was Dart, the skinny hunt-dog who had originally been part of the half wolf's Pack, before Sweet had taken over as Alpha and Terror's former Pack members had joined with them to make one big Pack.

But these dogs had never been truly happy in the Pack. They didn't like the way Alpha dealt with the awful things that were happening and felt that she favored the dogs she had known the longest. So they'd left to form their own group.

This must be where they're living now, Storm realized. *They haven't gotten very far from our camp, have they?*

She lowered herself closer to the ground—keeping the cheerful reunion in view, but herself out of sight. A terrible thought was racing across her mind.

If they're living so close to us, I wonder . . . could the bad dogs be from outside the Pack after all?

She craned her ears. *I have to know what they're planning.*

"It's been difficult," she heard Chase say, and Storm narrowed her eyes. *What's been difficult, Chase? Concealing your plans from Alpha? Hiding your treachery?*

"I'm sure it has." That was Rake. "I'm sorry we had to leave, but you can understand why, can't you?"

"Oh yes," said Chase softly, "and I don't blame you. Holding that territory with so few dogs is tough—and there's a lot more tension now."

"Still," broke in Dart, "the pups must be fun, and I guess they hold the Pack together. They must be growing up fast!"

"They're sweet," agreed Chase. "Breeze and Sunshine are both as crazy about them as their parent-dogs are. They do a lot of the pup-minding, which is helpful. But what about you four? How have you been doing?"

Oh, come on! thought Storm impatiently. *Enough with the chatter—I want to know about the conspiracy!*

"Well, we found this place for our camp," Woody was saying, "and it's worked really well. The only competition was a couple of raccoons. They were tougher opposition than I thought they'd be, but we chased them away eventually. See, Chase, there's a freshwater stream across this dip—can you hear it? The prey situation isn't bad, either."

"It's not as good as your camp," said Ruff, "but it suits us just fine. Tell me, how's Moon? And Thorn and Beetle?"

"I want to hear more about Breeze and her pup-minding," said Woody. "And about what you've been doing, too, Chase."

What? Storm pinned back her ears, frustrated. *This is just the kind of chat Lucky and I had with Bella and Arrow, when we visited them. It's all small dog-talk.*

For the first time, she felt a niggle of doubt in her belly. *Is that all Chase is doing? Catching up with her old friends?*

They'd soon get to talking about their plans, Storm reassured herself. She'd find out what their next attack would be, and when it would happen, and where. *All I have to do is wait. . . .*

She had to wait an interminable time. Once or twice she nearly dozed off as she listened to the five dogs gossip about their past

Packs and the dogs they had known. The snippets of news were the most tedious Storm had ever heard; no dog spoke of murder, or poison, or sabotage.

When Chase sprang to her paws, Storm thought she was finally about to reveal her plot. But all she did was share more friendly licks with her former comrades.

"It's been so good to see you all," she was saying. "And kind of relaxing, after all the trouble and stress in the Pack. I'll come again as soon as I can."

And with that, Chase turned and trotted back the way she'd come.

Storm almost yelped in surprise; she had to choke it back. It took her a moment to recover her wits, and with Chase quickly out of sight and earshot, she realized she'd have to hurry to catch up. *Was that all completely innocent? Really?*

It was too hard for Storm to believe. Picking up her paws, she began to run, determined not to let Chase out of her sight for longer than possible. *She could be doing anything while I can't see her. She could double back and talk quietly to her friends again. She could dodge me and get up to some terrible mischief—*

Panic rose in Storm's chest, making her heart thunder, and she forgot to be careful. Just as Chase's haunches came into view, both Storm's forepaws landed hard on a drift of dry leaves in a hollow, and as she lurched forward, she hit a twig. It snapped with a crack.

Chase spun around, her paws skidding on the earth. The small dog's eyes popped wide; Storm could see the whites of them in the dimness. She heard Chase's gasp, too, and saw her hackles spring up.

"Storm!" The small dog was breathing hard, and not from exertion. She backed slowly away, her legs trembling, but her rump banged against a pine trunk and she stifled a yelp. But she didn't take her eyes off Storm.

She looks terrified.

For a moment they gazed at each other in tense silence; then Chase whimpered, "Don't hurt me! *Please!*"

For a moment, Storm was too flummoxed to move or speak. Chase's whole body was shaking now; her fur was erect all over her hide.

Chase really *thinks I'm the bad dog!*

Storm licked her jaws; the simple act made Chase flinch and cower.

And if she truly believes I'm the traitor, Storm realized with thumping certainty, *it's not possible that she* is.

Chase couldn't be faking her abject terror; no dog could do that.

Oh, Sky-Dogs, thought Storm, with a sickening sensation in her gut. *I've been on the wrong trail. All this time I've wasted. It can't be Chase: I can see that she truly thinks it's me.*

But if not Chase, then who *had* killed Bruno and Whisper? The answer seemed to be further away from Storm than ever. *Right now it would be easier to catch the Golden Deer than to discover the traitor.*

"Chase! Chase, please." Storm stepped forward very carefully, feeling her own paws tremble. Chase had pressed herself hard against the trees that were blocking her escape; her lips were curled back from her teeth, but her eyes were still frenzied with fear. "I'm not going to hurt you, Chase, I promise. I'm not the traitor!"

"So you say. Stay back! Stay back, I warn you!"

"Chase, I'm not the bad dog." Storm dipped her head and pricked her ears, trying to look unthreatening. "I thought it was *you*! That's why I followed you in the first place!"

At last Chase's shaking began to subside. She narrowed her eyes, pinned back her ears, and gave a low, quivering growl. "You thought what? Storm, how *could* you?"

"I'm sorry. I can see now you're not guilty, or you wouldn't be so afraid of me." Storm risked another paw-pace toward the small dog, and this time Chase didn't wince; she looked more offended than scared.

"I'm not afraid! I—don't come any closer!" Chase's flanks heaved.

"I promise I won't hurt you. I swear on—on the Forest-Dog!" Storm pleaded.

Chase's eyes narrowed even farther. "All right," she said slowly. "All right, I'll believe that oath."

You're just not sure you believe me about anything else . . . realized Storm sadly. "We'll walk back to camp together. I won't even touch you. Come on."

Chase hesitated briefly, then gave a sharp nod. Keeping a dog-length between her flank and Storm's, she set off in the direction of the camp, one wary eye still flicking frequently toward Storm.

I'd best keep my word and my distance, thought Storm with a heavy heart. Carefully she made her way without letting even her tail swat Chase's rump by mistake. The silence as they walked together was the most awkward she'd ever experienced.

As they paused to scramble up a rocky slope, Chase flicked an ear at her and gave a low, warning snarl. "You'd better not tell any dog where Rake's camp is. I don't want them getting attacked by the bad dog too."

"All right," agreed Storm, as reassuringly as she could. "I won't tell. I've visited friends I miss, too."

Even confiding that secret didn't seem to affect Chase's attitude one bit; she still looked wary as she sprang up the slope, then turned very quickly to keep her eyes on Storm. She slunk on through the forest, halting to sniff the air as they drew nearer to the glade.

"I don't smell any Patrol Dogs," she growled.

"Maybe they're on the other side of the clearing," suggested Storm quickly. *Beetle and Thorn are supposed to be on patrol, but I'm not telling Chase that. They must have gone off by themselves again!*

The sky was already lightening, as the Sun-Dog yawned and stretched, when the two wanderers crept back into camp. They didn't exchange a word as they parted to go to their respective dens; Storm felt guilty and resentful all at once. *Chase was sneaking off in the middle of the night! What was I supposed to think? Of course I suspected her!*

There wasn't much time left to snatch some sleep, and uneasy dreams made Storm restless. Jumbled, horrible images kept startling her awake.

Chase, cornered and at bay, her rump against the tree; that fearful snarl widening and widening until suddenly the vicious, resentful face wasn't Chase's at all, but Terror's. The mad dog's eyes filling with blood; his jaws opening in a violent, shrieking howl. The savage brute lunging at Storm's throat. . . .

Storm woke so abruptly she was already springing to her paws. Dizzy, she trembled, blinking. *That howl is real! It's real!*

But it wasn't Terror's voice, or even Chase's, she realized as her senses returned. *It's Moon!*

The white-and-black Farm Dog was running into the glade as Storm wriggled out of her den. Lucky appeared from his own sleeping-place, and Sunshine, and Daisy too. Moon skidded to a halt on the grass, her eyes wide.

"I can't find Thorn and Beetle!" she yelped.

"What do you mean?" barked Lucky as the rest of the Pack began to scramble from their dens.

Moon's tail was as still as a tree trunk. "They never returned from patrol last night. . . . What if . . ." Now, her flanks began quivering. Storm could imagine the awful thoughts that were charging through her mind. "What if something's happened to them? What if they've met the traitor?"

CHAPTER FIFTEEN

The silence was so heavy, it was as though the Moon-Dog had placed her whole jaw on the head of every dog.

Storm's belly prickled with unease. *Was I wrong to keep my muzzle shut? Should I have told Moon, and Alpha, as soon as I saw what Beetle and Thorn were doing?*

Then she shook herself. Either way, there was nothing for it but to speak up now.

Storm took an abrupt pace forward. "Alpha . . . I might know where they are."

"What?" Alpha's expression was rigid with anger and disbelief as she stared at Storm.

Moon's face was even harder to look at as she echoed Alpha: "*What, Storm?*" There was a tremor of rage in her voice. "What do you know?"

Every dog's head had turned to watch. Storm swallowed hard. "We—Mickey and I—we saw Beetle and Thorn before—while we were on High Watch. They were prowling around the place where the longpaws are digging and building. I'm sure they're all right; they must have—"

"You *saw them*? What was the point of being on High Watch if you didn't report this?" Alpha's bark was dangerously high-pitched.

Moon bounded in front of Alpha to face Storm, her shoulders stiff with fear, her muzzle curled with aggression. "*Why didn't you say something?* Either of you?"

"I—Moon, it's my fault," stammered Storm "Mickey wanted to tell you, but I said no. I thought they'd be fine, they're such capable dogs, and they know the dangers—"

"That was *not* your decision to make!" howled Moon. "I could have stopped them!"

Storm felt the heat of shame rising in her chest. "I just didn't want to get them in trouble, not if they weren't doing anything bad. . . ." She saw Alpha give her an angry look and went on quickly. "I didn't want you all to go dashing after them if they had a good reason for—"

"*Of course* I would have gone after them! *They're my pups!*" Moon's

205

face was right in Storm's now, her eyes showing the whites, her fangs bared. "You've learned nothing! You made a decision that wasn't yours to make! And Thorn and Beetle *clearly aren't fine!*"

Storm swallowed again, dipping her head. What could she say? *Moon's right.* She forced herself to glance at Alpha, but the swift-dog's expression remained coldly furious. She had obviously decided to let Moon's fury do the barking, and she clearly agreed with every word her lead Patrol Dog was saying.

Storm opened her jaws to apologize, but the words wouldn't come. *What can I say? I was so wrong. I've committed the same crime twice, proved Alpha was right not to trust me. . . .*

"Packmates." It was Lucky who stepped forward, his face stern. "We can discuss the rights and wrongs of this later." From the look he shot Storm, though, it was clear where he thought the wrongs lay. "Right now we need to go after Beetle and Thorn. No more delays!"

"You're right, Beta," said Alpha. Her voice was too level and cold, as if she was repressing a need to bite some dog.

"I'll take out a party to search for them, and rescue them if necessary." Lucky raised his head to look around at the closest dogs.

"I'm coming, of course." Moon shot a venomous glare at Storm. "They are *my pups.*"

"And I'll come," said Storm, averting her eyes from Moon's.

"Me too." Mickey sounded subdued, but his shoulders quivered with determination.

"And me." Breeze padded into the circle.

Lucky nodded. "That will have to do. There's no time to waste."

"The rest of us will search the other side of our territory, closer to the Endless Lake," said Alpha. "Just in case they went that way instead. Good luck, my Beta."

Lucky sprang into a run, and the other dogs of the party followed at his heels as he raced into the forest. Storm could barely feel the snap of twigs and the crackle of leaves beneath her paws; her head swam with horror at the thought of what she might have done. She could only focus on Lucky's golden haunches, and keep running, and try not to think. She was aware of Mickey close behind her, and she couldn't help wondering how he was feeling now. *Terrible, I guess. And that's my fault too.* Breeze and Moon were farther back, the gentle brown dog staying close to the anxious, wounded Mother-Dog. Guilt made Storm gather speed, keeping her well ahead of them; maybe it was as much fear of Moon as desperation to get to Beetle and Thorn.

"I can't imagine how worried Moon is," muttered Lucky as Storm bounded abreast of him. "I never really understood the bond parent-dogs have with their pups until I had a litter of my own. There's nothing more important than your pups, nothing. If anything happened to mine—" He fell silent and ran even faster.

Despite the heat of her shame, Storm felt a deeper stab of sadness that made her catch her breath. *His own pups are far more important to Lucky than I ever was,* she realized. *Is that what he's telling me? Of course they are. It's natural.*

But it still hurts.

As the search party broke out of the final line of trees, Lucky slowed the pace, lowering his body so that the long meadow grass would give him cover. Beside him, Storm followed his lead; she heard the others' pawsteps slow, and the rustle of the undergrowth as they slunk across the meadow.

Something tickled the sensitive flesh inside Storm's nostrils: something familiar. *That's Thorn's scent!* Close behind it, she detected Beetle's, too.

"Lucky," she murmured, pausing to sniff at the air. "Lucky, I smell them both. They did come this way."

Lucky retraced his steps and lowered his muzzle to the ground at Storm's paws. "Yes," he agreed, "and the trail's heading for the longpaw site, just as you said." He shot Storm a disapproving look but said no more. That didn't reassure Storm. *He's only holding back until Thorn and Beetle are found.*

As Moon and Breeze caught up to them, Moon's eyes widened at her pups' scent, and her ears pricked and trembled.

"Thorn . . ." she whispered. "Beetle."

Lucky gave her a reassuring nuzzle. "We're close to them. Come on," he said softly. "Every dog behind me. We'll approach the site in single file, so we disturb the grass as little as possible. We'll have your pups back in no time, Moon. I promise."

Hunching himself low, Lucky turned and slunk with cautious pawsteps toward the first gash of raw earth and a line of new-looking tall metal stakes. Storm fell in behind, feeling her heart begin to race with what seemed like unreasonable, tearing anxiety.

I know what it is, she realized abruptly. *I know why this feels even more terrible than it should. It reminds me of the day we set out to rescue Fiery. We were just this full of hope, just as confident we could rescue him and get him to safety.* Cold fear shuddered down her spine. *I hope we're luckier this time. . . .*

As they drew closer to the shiny metal poles, Storm could see a net of crisscrossed wire between them; it was a complete barrier that blocked their way. But the trail of Beetle and Thorn didn't stop at the fence, so the searching dogs couldn't either.

"I saw a hole . . ." Storm told Lucky as she snuffled at the base of the wire. "Here."

Lucky came to her shoulder, and both dogs studied the turned earth. It was rawer and darker even than the paths of the great loudcages: The soil had been clawed out very recently. At the base of the fence, the wire was slightly twisted and warped, as if a sizable dog had squirmed beneath it.

"This is where they went through," murmured Lucky.

"Then so will we." At his shoulder, Moon looked tense and determined. Before Lucky could so much as growl a warning, the white-and-black Farm Dog had pushed past him and plunged into the hole. Her haunches wriggled briefly, and she emerged on the other side of the wire, shaking earth from her coat.

"All right," said Lucky softly. "Let's follow Moon."

One by one the rest of the party squeezed through the tight gap, shook off the loose mud, then paused to look around for dangers. Storm came last, following Breeze; she couldn't help flinching as she spotted a giant loudcage not a rabbit-chase away.

Every dog held their breath, but the massive yellow creature was as still as death; no growl or breath came from it. Behind and beside it were others of its kind; every single one was motionless, lifeless.

"Don't let that fool you," growled Lucky. "They're not dead. And they wake up fast. Let's be very careful—just because we can't hear longpaws doesn't mean they're not close."

Storm's hide prickled beneath her fur as the dogs picked their way between the slumbering yellow beasts and the great piles of gravel and sand the longpaws had left. The stink of the longpaws was very strong and their traces were everywhere: paw prints, loudcage-tracks, great gouged holes that made astonishingly straight and level lines in the earth. Breeze stretched her neck to sniff at a pile of metal rods; she leaped back almost at once with a suppressed yelp of alarm.

"The stink of all this stuff," she growled in frustration. "What in the Earth-Dog's name is it all for? It's so hard to pick up Beetle and Thorn's trail."

"No, it isn't," whispered Storm, treading nervously closer to a loudcage. Her paws shook, but she had to get closer. There was something . . .

"Storm," Breeze murmured, "what are you doing? You shouldn't get too close to it."

"I think it's okay," Lucky told her. "Loudcages don't move if their longpaws don't make them."

"Weird . . ." Breeze sounded no more confident, but Storm ignored her. She got right up next to the loudcage.

"Yes!" she exclaimed, a rasp of fear in her throat. "Smell this loudcage's paws!"

The paws were huge, round, and black, softer than the loudcages' metal bodies, and they alone were taller than any of the dogs. Storm risked a glance up at the beast; it didn't stir, even when she touched her trembling nose to its paw. The stench of it was strong, mixed up with scents of earth and mud, but there was something else, unmistakable.

Beside Storm, Moon gave a low snarl, her hackles rising. "Beetle. He hasn't just touched this. *He marked it.*"

Storm's eyes widened. Moon was right. Sniffing again, she found Thorn's scent beneath her brother's.

Moon scampered to the next loudcage and put her nostrils to its giant feet. "And this one!" she growled. "They've marked all these loudcages, deliberately. Reckless young *fools!*"

Moon's voice was full of fear as well as fury. "When I find you two, you're in for the scolding of your lives!"

"Then let's find them, Moon, and get them out of here." Lucky was calm and resolute, but there was an undercurrent of anger in his voice, too.

I may have been an idiot to keep it to myself, thought Storm. *But really—those two should have known much better than to come here at all, let alone mark it as their territory.*

Now that the search dogs had found the markings, the trail was easy to follow, in spite of the powerful longpaw scents that pervaded everything. They crept on through the site, sniffing at fences and piles of wood and upturned buckets, finding evidence of Beetle's and Thorn's markings everywhere they went. Although Moon was limping quite badly now, she was moving ahead of the others, her nose more certain of her pups' trail than any dog's.

Moon came to a standstill beneath yet another sleeping loudcage. She stared up at it, seeming unafraid, yet the whites showed around her blue eyes. Her shoulders trembled as the others joined her.

"The trail: It stops here," she growled. Her voice rose on a tide of panic till it was a frenzied yelp. "I can't smell anything but longpaws. *Where are my pups?*"

Every dog froze. "Moon, no!" growled Lucky. "We have to be quiet!"

But Moon could contain herself no longer. *"Where are they?!"*

For a horrible moment every dog stood rigid with fear, waiting for the trampling, rushing tread of longpaws. But there was nothing. Into the silence came a sound that made Storm's hackles rise; then she recognized it.

Barking. Desperate, muffled barking. *Beetle! Thorn!*

"This way!" exclaimed Storm, and bounded toward the sound with the others at her heels.

She skidded to a halt on a patch of drier, dusty earth. Before her was a squat, square longpaw den on wheels. As Storm hesitated, Moon lurched past her, then halted, eyeing the small den with fear.

"Beetle!" she barked. "Thorn!"

Another volley of familiar barks came from inside the den's metal walls. "We're here! In here!"

Moon gasped, terrified, as did Breeze beside her, but Lucky and Mickey bounded confidently up to the den. Lucky even rose onto his hind legs and placed his forepaws on the metal wall.

Of course, thought Storm, *he was a Lone Dog, and Mickey was a Leashed Dog. They might know just how to get inside this den.* Storm tilted her head, staring in perplexity at the weird hybrid thing. *No shining clear-stone eyes, like a loudcage has, but it definitely has loudcage-paws. Maybe its head has been chopped off by the longpaws. Why would they do that?*

But there was no time to think about why longpaws would need a headless loudcage. Moon seemed to know that, too; she crept up to the beast's belly, terror in her eyes. *She's thinking of Fiery,* realized Storm.

"Are you all right, pups?" she whined anxiously. "Have they hurt you?"

"We're fine, fine!" Thorn's voice was muffled by the walls, but her bark sounded strong. "The longpaws shut us in here, but they haven't harmed us yet!"

Moon closed her eyes, looking shaky with relief. But she quickly opened them again. "How will we get them out?" she muttered to Lucky.

Storm paced up and down, examining the walls of the den and sniffing at the metal. "We could try to break a hole in the wall? If we all ran at it together, we might get through."

Lucky shook his head. "No, that won't work, Storm. But I know what to do."

He padded to a hatch in the wall, one with straight sides; there was some kind of silver-colored stick attached to it. Every dog watched, dumbfounded, as Lucky reared up on his hind legs again, stretching high. He scrabbled with his paws at the jutting silver thing, finally catching it.

And he tugged.

It clicked down easily, rotating on its end. As if the Sky-Dogs had run at it from the inside, the hatch swung wide open sideways, banging against the wall.

Lucky jumped back, grinning, but Moon was already racing past him. Despite her injured paw, she sprang up into the den with a yelp of joy.

Storm caught a glimpse of what was inside: Beetle and Thorn, straining toward their Mother-Dog, but held by ropes around their necks. There was barely time to register this new problem, though. An earsplitting shriek tore the air, a terrible wailing sound that no dog could have made. Every dog flinched and froze in terror, crouching low to the ground, but the deafening noise didn't stop. On and on it went, an appalling howl that could scramble a dog's brain.

The headless loudcage was calling the longpaws!

CHAPTER SIXTEEN

I want to run. I need to run. It was all Storm could think through the screeching sound that was battering her skull. She shut her eyes tightly and clenched her jaws.

But I must not run!

She forced herself to stay in her place, digging her claws into the ground, every muscle rigid and taut. *I must not run! Beetle and Thorn are still tied up in there—they can't run!*

Through the shrieking wail, something else was in her ears, a reassuring sound. *Lucky's voice.*

"Don't be scared." He was barking now, calm but insistent. "That sound can't hurt you, and neither can the den-thing. It's calling for its longpaws, that's all. It's what they do when you disturb them. Don't panic."

Storm felt her heart begin to slow; she was able to think again, though her brain still hammered with the ongoing, wailing racket. Breeze too seemed less terror-struck, and Mickey looked wide-eyed but steady.

"But it does mean the longpaws will come soon," Lucky went on. "We need to get Beetle and Thorn out of here, and fast!" He leaped up into the den hatch, vanishing inside just as Moon had.

It went against all Storm's instincts to follow him in there, but she fought against them. Tensing every muscle, clenching her jaw till it hurt, she crouched and sprang up into the belly of the beast.

It took a moment for her eyes to adjust to the dimness, but she quickly made out Beetle and Thorn. The two stood against the far wall, eagerly facing their rescuers, their tails quivering. Both dogs strained against the rope collars that fastened them to round metal hooks in the wall. Before them, on the ground, sat bowls of water and dry pieces of food that looked untouched. Moon stood by them, tugging helplessly on Thorn's rope with her teeth.

"Storm!" barked Beetle. "Lucky! You came!"

"Breeze and Mickey!" yelped Thorn with joy.

"We came, but we'll have to be quick," growled Lucky. "The longpaws are already on their way."

Thorn shook her head violently, snarling at the bite of the rope. "We tried to get loose, but these are too tight."

"I can't do anything," whined Moon. "They don't yield to teeth."

"And we can't break the ropes," added Beetle in frustration. "They're too strong."

"Backward," barked Lucky sharply.

Moon gave a snarl of belated realization. "Of course! Try that, my pups. You have to wriggle backward, like Lucky says." She fastened her teeth around the loop of rope on Beetle's neck. "Pull back now."

She lowered her hindquarters, straining hard with stiff forelegs as Beetle struggled and writhed. The rope slipped a little toward his jaw.

"Pull harder!" Moon demanded, urgency overcoming the fear in her voice.

Clenching his jaw, Beetle dragged his head backward, twisting and yanking. The rope moved slowly, jerkily, toward his ear. Moon gave a low growl and hauled harder on the collar, her paws slipping.

Lucky was already doing the same thing for Thorn, his teeth sunk into the rope collar as she strained backward. As Storm turned anxiously to watch him, she heard a thump and a clatter. When she spun back, Moon was spitting out the rope collar, and

Beetle was dancing in a circle, as well as he could in the small space. "You did it, Moon!"

Lucky was still fighting with the rope on Thorn's neck; Thorn's eyes were wide and white-rimmed as she wrenched herself backward, claws scrabbling. Nervously Storm twisted to peer out of the door. "We have to hurry!" she growled.

"What's in the bowls?" Mickey was sniffing at the dry food. "It smells good—didn't you want to eat?"

Moon shot him a look of disbelief; Storm raised her brows. Beetle gave a yelp of disgust. "We don't touch longpaw food!"

Thorn gasped and snarled as she struggled. "Longpaws—killed—poisoned our—Father-Dog!"

Mickey hesitated for a moment, then cocked an ear in the direction of the bowls. He gave them another sniff, then hunched his shoulders and began to wolf down the nuggets of food.

Thorn's rope snapped away, whipping her muzzle, and she staggered backward, shaking her head. At just that moment, through the hatch entrance, Storm saw two pairs of gleaming bright-white eyes, jolting across the ground toward them. They flooded the muddy ground with light.

"Longpaws! They're here!"

All of the dogs spun toward the entry hatch. Mickey gulped

down the last mouthful of food and growled. Then, at the same moment, they all sprang for the way out, bumping one another's flanks as they hurried to escape.

Storm emerged first from the chaos, her forepaws landing hard on the earth, and she bounded forward, leading the way toward the ragged hole in the fence. She could hear the pounding paws of the others as they ran behind her; *we're going to make it!*

Her ears twitched and swiveled as she ran. It was hard to count the pawsteps running behind her, but she didn't dare pause to glance over her shoulder. The glowing eyes of the loudcages were bumping and weaving toward them, but the fence was nearly in reach.

Then, horribly, she heard another sound: a hollow thud, and a yelp of distress.

Storm skidded to a halt, her claws sending up a shower of loose earth. All her companions were still behind her, slowing in confusion—

But not Breeze!

Storm turned and raced back between her comrades. She saw the dark pool of shadow in the ground almost immediately: a deep hole that she—and they—had only avoided by blind luck. Storm crept to its edge. Breeze was a slightly paler shadow in the bottom of the pit, her eyes staring up at Storm in panic, the whites showing. The brown dog stood up on her hindpaws and scrabbled frantically at the earth walls.

"Help me! Storm, help!"

The rest of the party had turned back now and were gathered around Storm, yelping in dismay.

"Hold on, Breeze," Storm growled. "Don't panic. It's not too deep at all." *Just too deep for a dog Breeze's size to climb out . . .* "We'll help you!"

Taking a deep breath, trying not to think about the approaching loudcages and their increasing roar, Storm jumped down into the hole next to Breeze. She nuzzled the smaller dog's neck, trying to reassure her panicking friend.

"Keep calm. I'll push you up." Storm raised her head and barked to Lucky and Mickey, who were peering over the edge. "Be ready to pull her!"

The two dogs crouched at the edge of the drop. Storm lowered her head and pushed at Breeze's shaking hindquarters, shoving as hard as she could as Breeze clawed desperately at the sheer sides. Earth crumbled and Breeze whimpered, but gradually she was scrambling higher.

"The longpaws," came Thorn's whimper from beyond the edge of the hole. "They're nearly here!"

"Hurry, hurry!" yelped Beetle.

I will, thought Storm irritably, *if you'll all just shut up!* Gritting her teeth, she heaved again, harder, jolting Breeze up another few worm-lengths. Breeze's hindquarters were in her face, and her lashing tail almost blinded Storm.

Then, abruptly, her weight was lifted away. Lucky had the brown dog by the scruff of her neck and was hauling hard, with Mickey's help. Breeze was pulled up and away, and Storm heard her land with a soft thump on safe ground.

Panting, turning a full circle, Storm glanced around the hole. There was no room for a running start; she would just have to spring for it.

"Come on, Storm," barked Lucky. "I'll pull you up, too."

"Oh, *hurry!*" yelped Moon.

Crouching, coiling herself tightly, Storm clenched her jaws. When every muscle was bunched tight, she pushed away with her hindquarters and sprang toward safety.

Lucky bared his jaws and opened them, ready to catch her by the scruff, but his help wasn't necessary. She was clear of the hole by a tail-length as she landed on all four paws.

"Thank you, Storm," panted Breeze, her sides heaving. "Thank you!"

"Never mind that now—let's *go!*" Storm bounded toward the fence but stood back as the others dived for the hole and scrabbled through. Moon was last, after her rescued pups, except for Lucky. He waited, nodding impatiently at Storm.

"Go on, Storm! As Beta, I should take the rear."

There were barks from the longpaws now, and the screeching noise of loudcages drawing to a halt. As pounding longpaw feet ran toward the fence, Storm twisted and shoved herself through the hole in the wire.

When she emerged on the other side she turned, looking desperately for Lucky, but he was already halfway through the gap. He hauled himself out, barking, *"Run!"*

The longpaws were running now, too, but they were on the other side of the fence and they carried no loudsticks. Dizzy with relief, Storm spun and raced at her Beta's flank, back toward the safety of their camp.

CHAPTER SEVENTEEN

The pale golden, early light of the Sun-Dog glowed between the pine trunks as the dogs crashed through the undergrowth and back into the clearing. Panting, they all came to a halt as they blinked at Alpha. She was standing on all four paws, worry still etched on her face as her pups gamboled between her slender legs. Watching her eyes, Storm could tell she was counting the members of the rescue party, over and over again. At last Alpha nodded, her expression one of satisfaction and deep relief, and all her muscles seemed to relax. She sat back on her haunches.

"You did it," she said quietly. "Well done, all of you. And welcome back, Thorn and Beetle." Her greeting to the two wanderers was tinged with the promise, Storm thought, of further stern words to come later. But for now, their Alpha was clearly too happy to have her Pack back together—whole; no dog lost.

The rest of the Pack was gathering, yelping with delight. "What happened?" asked Daisy.

"Where did you find them?" yapped Sunshine. "Oh, it's so good to have you *all* back!"

It was Moon who stepped forward, her stiff tail quivering, her eyes flashing with anger. "My pups—*my offspring*—decided it would be a clever idea to go to the place where the longpaws are building. They thought it showed intelligence to go and mess up that place, as some kind of ridiculous revenge." The growl in her voice grew louder, more threatening. "And they did all this *after I had told them* to stay away from there—to stay away from *all* long-paws. And I apologize to the whole Pack on behalf of my stupid, irresponsible litter!"

The Pack stood silent, shuffling and blinking in shock and slight embarrassment. It was so unlike Moon to criticize her pups, thought Storm—especially with such savage words. *She must be really furious. It's clear they terrified her with this escapade of theirs.*

"Moon! That's not fair!" protested Beetle. "All we wanted to do was make the longpaws leave! We thought if we made a mess at their building-place, they'd go away!"

"And we deserve revenge," barked Thorn grumpily. "The longpaws killed our Father-Dog and they should pay."

"That is exactly my point, you foolish pups!" Moon turned on the pair of them. "They killed your Father-Dog, the strongest, smartest, *best* dog I ever knew. Fiery was the most powerful fighter our Pack ever had. What did you two think *you* could achieve? What was the point of putting yourselves in such needless danger? You're still young! You don't have the strength your Father-Dog had—and you're certainly not as smart, judging by your antics today!"

Thorn and Beetle stared moodily at the ground, their tails clamped to their haunches, their ears drooping. There was sullen resentment in their posture, but it was clear they were cowed by their Mother-Dog's words.

They know what they did was wrong, Storm thought. *They may not ever admit it, but Moon's made it pretty clear how stupid and reckless they've been. They know.*

"Tell me exactly what happened," said Alpha, her voice level. She seemed to have decided that for the moment at least, no more scolding was needed from her, after the tongue-lashing the two had had from Moon.

"We just wanted to mess things up a bit," mumbled Beetle. "But two longpaws caught us. They grabbed Thorn, and I was furious and I went to help her—but they were cunning and strong and they grabbed me too."

"That was always going to happen," snapped Moon.

Thorn tucked her ears back, looking ashamed. "And they tied us up, with rope around our necks so we couldn't get away."

There were gasps from the Pack, especially from the dogs who had never been Leashed in their lives. "Tied you up?" barked Snap in horror.

"Lucky knew what to do," said Mickey, nodding respectfully at his Beta.

"It wasn't hard, once we knew where Beetle and Thorn were." Lucky paced forward. "It was the kind of den I knew how to open. And ropes can be wriggled out of, if a dog has help and can keep its nerve. The worst part was getting away from there, once the den sounded the alarm and the longpaws came running."

"Yes." Breeze nodded vigorously. "That was frightening. I fell into a hole while I was running, and Storm had to get me out." She wagged her tail gratefully at Storm.

Gradually the muttering and the shocked explanations died away, as Alpha remained silent. At last she stepped forward, waving her tail slowly and thoughtfully. Her face was stern.

"I agree with Moon," she told them all. She shot Beetle and Thorn a disapproving glance. "These two pups of hers ran willingly into a perilous situation, and by doing so they put the whole Pack in danger. And that danger has not gone away; what if the longpaws come looking for them now?"

That did not seem to have occurred to Beetle and Thorn. They exchanged a look of dawning horror, and their heads hung low.

There was movement at Alpha's paws; the pups had abandoned their halfhearted game, clearly sensing the seriousness of the adult dogs around them. Storm could see Tiny, cowering behind her Mother-Dog's legs, her eyes huge. The pups surely did not understand the gravity of the Pack's situation, but she could tell they knew that the older dogs were on edge—nervous.

It would be so tough on all the pups if we have to leave this camp now, she thought. *And it would be especially hard on Tiny. She's the most vulnerable of the four of them. . . . And they'd be even more vulnerable if we didn't have a camp. . . .*

Alpha's loud bark broke into her thoughts. She glared at Thorn and Beetle. "You two were irresponsible and stupid to go to the longpaw place."

Neither of the litter-siblings said a word, but they crouched low, clearly knowing that their only choice was humble submission.

"What's more," Alpha went on, "it was equally irresponsible and stupid for Storm and Mickey to conceal what they knew about your no-sun jaunts. All four of you will be punished."

Again, thought Storm, gloomily and rather resentfully. *Always, I get punished. When I'm just trying to do the right thing . . .*

Alpha was still talking in that severe, disapproving voice; Storm wished that she would just get on with the punishment. "Mickey and Beetle will take High Watch together. When their watch is finished, Storm and Thorn can take over. You can all use the time to reflect on how irresponsible you are. And maybe, if you have older dogs close by, you won't be so eager to run off and put the whole Pack at risk!"

The earth between her claws was raw and moist . . . the stench of loudcages clung to her nose like a vicious claw. All around her was darkness, except for where those strange longpaw-lights shone down in pools of glaring whiteness. Strips of metal, pale planks of freshly cut wood, and shining longpaw tools lay all around, in heaps and stacks; she flinched away from them in fear. And there, right in her line of vision, was the metal den on wheels where Beetle and Thorn had been caged. It looked bigger and more intimidating than it had before, and the longpaw-lights bathed it in a sinister white glow.

How can I be back at the longpaw camp? *Storm wondered. Oh,*

Sky-Dogs, Alpha will be so furious with me. . . .

With shaking paws, she trod toward the light of the den, feeling herself slip in the damp, turned mud. The hatch was there in the wall, with its silver lever; as Storm stared at it, she could hear the barks of the dogs imprisoned within. But they didn't sound like Beetle and Thorn; the yelps were high-pitched and terrified, the squeaking cries of tiny helpless creatures. . . .

It's the pups! They've been captured!

Storm lunged for the hatch, scrabbling at the lever. But the trick that had worked instantly for Lucky proved impossible for her. The silver thing slipped from beneath her paws, or stuck fast, however hard she tried to grab and turn it. Her teeth slid off its surface, making her stumble and bang her skull against the metal side of the den. Once again she scratched wildly at the lever with her claws, but it would not turn. She bit down on it, pulling with her jaws—but succeeded only in tearing out her own teeth.

It's no good. I can't open it. I can't help the pups!

There was a roaring sound behind her. Wild-eyed, Storm turned to see the glaring eyes of the longpaws' loudcages, bumping across the ground toward her. It's too late!

Then she realized the loudcages weren't bumping at all. They were flying across the ground, faster and faster. She'd never seen loudcages move so swiftly. They raced toward her as if they had wings. . . .

And then she saw. They were not loudcages at all; there was only one pair of *glowing eyes, and those belonged to a dog. A great, black, terrifying creature that thundered toward her and the imprisoned pups. It was almost upon her, a hulking beast made of shadow and terror.*

The Fear-Dog.

Storm could not move, could not bark. She was as powerless as the pups that she could not save. Frozen, helpless, she watched the Fear-Dog loom over her, its jaws falling open to reveal deadly fangs and an endless, gaping throat. . . .

She woke, shuddering, her racing heart pumping blood through her veins that felt like ice water.

The Fear-Dog.

The longpaw site.

And one of them, at least, was real.

Staggering to her paws, Storm stared around her. Against a gray sky, pale at the horizon with the promise of the waking Sun-Dog, she saw the walls and trenches and loudcages of the longpaws' building-place. Storm swallowed hard, suppressing a whine.

I walked in my sleep again. And this place is wide awake!

The longpaw site was a chaos of activity. The giant yellow loud-cages growled and rumbled and screeched, digging deep grooves in the earth, or shoving piles of mud and stones. Longpaws barked and yelled to one another, and hammered metal spikes with great clubs of iron. Even more of those huge square pits had been dug in the earth; vast piles of excavated soil dotted the ground like small, newborn mountains. Turning, Storm saw more loudcages approaching from her own side of the wire fence; they looked purposeful and determined, grumbling and growling toward the site.

Alpha was right. More longpaws are coming! They want this place for themselves, and they'll keep it no matter what we do. How could Beetle and Thorn ever have believed they could stop them?

A loudcage roared to life, barely a rabbit-chase from her flank, and Storm leaped into the air in fright. She had been too disoriented to notice it lying there in wait, and now it was attacking her!

Camp! I have to get back to the camp! Spinning, she fled, but the ground was uneven and her head was still dizzy, and she stumbled. She had barely gotten back to her paws when the loudcage was upon her.

With a bark of pure terror, she tried to leap to freedom and safety, but there was no escape. Storm felt herself engulfed by a great metal maw. She slithered back, whining with terror.

Metal bars were in front of her, and at both her flanks. Something thudded onto her back and she struggled wildly. *No! This can't be happening!* The growling of the hungry loudcage filled her ears, throbbed inside her head. *It's eating me!*

From somewhere in her addled, terror-stricken brain, a memory came to her. Moon's urgent voice, barking an instruction to help free Beetle and Thorn: *You have to wriggle backward!*

Would it work for a ravenous loudcage the way it did for a rope? *I have to try!*

Desperately she struggled and writhed backward, claws raking the base of the cage, haunches straining. She flattened herself as the cage constricted around her. She kicked back, fighting it, shoving herself with her forepaws now. Her hindclaws found purchase on a hard edge, and she gave a final massive wrench of her muscles, scraping her spine against metal.

She was flung backward into free space and crashed to the earth with an ungainly thump, showering herself in loose soil. *I'm out!*

There was no time to glory in her escape. Rolling over, scrambling upright, she sprang past a barking longpaw, dodged another that lunged for her, then bolted for the forest and for freedom.

CHAPTER EIGHTEEN

The Sun-Dog was a low, golden dazzle between the trees as Storm dragged her aching paws into the camp. She let herself feel a shiver of relief at being home and safe and unseen; the feeling lasted until a stern voice growled her name.

Storm's heart plummeted. *Lucky.*

He stood on the grass of the clearing, watching her, and he did not look happy. His ears were low, his tail still, and his eyes were dark and displeased.

"Beta." She decided the respect of formality was her best option.

"Where have you been?" When she didn't answer, he stalked forward, studying her from nose to tailtip. "What do you think you're up to, wandering about during no-sun when you're not on patrol? Do you have any idea how bad this looks for you?"

Despite her exhaustion, Storm felt her hackles bristle. "I don't care how it *looks*. I went to the longpaw site. And there are *lots* more longpaws around than before."

"*What?*" Lucky's eyes widened. "You deliberately went to the longpaw place again?"

"No," Storm murmured. "Well, not exactly. I—"

She had no time to think of a way to explain it; Lucky's yelp of disbelief had woken some of the other Pack members, and they were crawling from their dens, shaking themselves, yapping and growling to one another in confusion.

"What's going on?" Snap blinked. "Did I hear right?"

Daisy shook herself as if she was trying to rid herself of sleepiness. "Storm went back to the longpaw place?"

"Wait, no! I—I didn't disobey orders or anything." Storm glanced guiltily around at her Packmates. "It wasn't delib— I mean, I didn't plan to—" She swallowed hard. "Look, it doesn't matter why I went there! What matters is that there are *lots* more longpaws now! Everything we worried about, everything we feared—it's happening!"

They all stared at her, but not as if they were interested in heeding her warning. There was disbelief in their eyes, and shock, and more than a little disapproval. In the middle of the awkward silence, Alpha stalked from her den and came to a halt in front of Storm.

"What do I have to do, Storm?" she growled. "What do I have to say to you to get you to stay in line? You are a Pack Dog! And Pack Dogs respect Pack orders!"

"But, Alpha—"

"Quiet!" Alpha's lip curled back from her teeth. "You are walking on very thin ice. And you have not heard the end of this, Storm—Beta, Third Dog, and I will be discussing your attitude. In the meantime, make yourself useful. Get up to High Watch and relieve Mickey and Beetle, *as you've been ordered.*"

Storm's tail and ears drooped, and she stared at the ground, torn between shame, embarrassment, and pure, hot rage. *I should explain. Maybe now is the time to tell them all about my sleepwalking. How else can I convince them that I didn't mean to do this?*

But what would I say? That I wander around during no-sun, while I'm fast asleep, with no idea of where I'm going and what I'm up to? That will only make things much worse.

Defeated, miserable, and resentful, she turned without another word and plodded out of the glade and onto the path that led to High Watch. She heard another dog run to her side and knew from her scent that it was her fellow sentry, Thorn, but she didn't turn to look at her.

She heard the bark that followed Thorn, though. It was Moon, calling a warning to her daughter:

"Be *careful*, Thorn. Keep your eyes and your nose open!"

Storm's breath caught in her throat, and her heart turned over. Even after all that had happened since she'd gotten back to camp, she still felt hurt. Moon didn't warn them *both* to be careful—she was telling Thorn to be wary of one threat only: Storm herself.

I saved Thorn, thought Storm, as grief and loneliness settled in her belly like a stone. *Not only that, I saved Alpha's pups—I saved the whole future of this Pack.*

And they still don't trust me.

"I don't understand why *you* would go back to the longpaws' place," Thorn was saying as she walked at Storm's side. "After Beetle and I got into such trouble? It was *our* idea to go and threaten the long-paws, and we got the tongue-whipping from Alpha, and then *you* think it's a good idea to go and do the same?"

Storm said nothing; she was too busy trying to control her temper.

"And you did it *right afterward!* It's not like you have a bigger right to go there than me and Beetle. It was *our* Father-Dog the longpaws killed. What were you thinking?"

I am going to turn around and bite her in a moment, thought Storm grimly. *Yet that's the one thing I absolutely can't do.* She clamped her jaws together tightly and stalked on up the cliff path, every sinew taut and trembling with the strain of keeping control.

"*We're* the ones who should be attacking them, not you!" Thorn's petulant voice was like a buzzing mosquito in her ears; Storm would have loved to swat her off the cliff with a paw. "The longpaws aren't *your* problem, and now you've made Alpha even angrier, and it will be even harder for us to get revenge for our Father-Dog."

Even through the heat of her anger, Storm realized one thing very clearly: All of Alpha's scolding, all the punishment she'd inflicted on Beetle and Thorn, was for nothing. Thorn was plainly still determined to do something about the longpaws, and that must mean Beetle was too. They hadn't been warned off at all. *Those two aren't even a little bit grateful that I helped rescue them,* thought Storm angrily and with a horrible undercurrent of dread. *They just see me as some dog who thwarted their plans. They're idiots, both of them!*

Thorn still hadn't shut up by the time they reached High Watch and settled down to keep guard. *I'd have thought ignoring her would put her off, but she's too fanatical about the whole longpaw problem,* Storm realized with a roll of her eyes.

"You watch the Endless Lake," she snapped at last, when Thorn paused for breath. "I'll keep watch on the land side."

With Thorn's complaints still battering her ears, Storm tried to turn away and stare determinedly inland. It was hard to ignore the nagging, but she could try.

The trouble was, if she'd wanted to take her mind off things, Storm had chosen the wrong direction. Far below, the longpaws' building-place was bustling with activity. The fence had been opened at one side, and a stream of small loudcages poured in, while the much bigger, noisier yellow loudcages plowed and grooved the earth inside. The longpaws on foot looked like a swarm of insects; they wore yellow fur, and even brighter yellow coverings on their heads. It all reminded Storm of the relentless busyness of bees around a hive. Even at this distance she could hear their purposeful barks.

They know exactly what they want and what they're doing, thought Storm. *I wish I did. It's so vital to the Pack and our future that we find out what these longpaws are up to.*

Why couldn't Lucky have listened? Storm lay down, her head on her paws, and sighed deeply as she watched the site. *He used to listen to me. He used to trust my instincts. He used to trust me. And all that wasn't so long ago. What happened?*

She was ignoring Thorn's muttering, to the point where it was as incomprehensible as the distant barking of the longpaws. It was an apparently endless whine about *Beetle and me* and *Father-Dog* and *longpaws* and *vengeance* and *it's not fair.*

"How was that supposed to help any dog? 'Ooh, we're all in terrible danger.'" Thorn's voice was high and indignant, scraping on the inside of Storm's skull. "Were you *trying* to sound like you were making threats?"

Storm didn't even know what happened then, only that the last thin rope that was holding her fury in place snapped. She was suddenly up on all four paws, her sluggish misery shattered, snarling viciously into Thorn's face.

"What's that? How was I helping? You mean, how dare I care about the Pack? How dare I try to keep every dog safe? You tell me, Thorn. *You tell me.* Tell me about the last time I hurt any dog in our Pack! When was it? *When did I hurt any of the Pack Dogs?*"

Thorn wasn't answering. Through the red mist of her rage, Storm became aware that Thorn was cowering, quivering, her wide eyes locked on Storm's and filled with terror. She lay flat, crouched tight against the ground; Storm herself was standing over her, forepaws splayed on either side of her head. Something dripped onto Thorn's petrified face; Storm realized it was slaver from her own snarling jaws.

What am I doing?!

Blinking, Storm drew back—though for all the will of the Forest-Dog, she could not uncurl her muzzle. Her eyes stayed locked on Thorn as the smaller dog shivered, crept a little closer, then rolled to show her belly. Thorn's tongue hung sideways from her dry mouth, and the whites were visible all around her dark eyes as she whimpered, "I'm sorry. Sorry, Storm."

"No." Storm licked her jaws, forcing herself to cover her fangs. "No, *I'm* sorry. I wasn't attacking you, Thorn."

"I—I know, Storm." Thorn's voice trembled as she rolled back onto her belly and crawled clear. "It's fine. No offense taken. Sorry." Her eyes did not once leave Storm.

"I didn't mean to scare you—"

"No! No, I know! It's all right. I went too far. I'm sorry." Thorn was gabbling now as she sat up, her tail tucked tightly around her haunches. *"Sorry."*

And even as she wriggled around to face the Endless Lake once more, Thorn was *still* eyeing Storm sidelong, her expression full of nervous fear.

Storm shook herself. *I must not lose control like that! I must not....*

She sat on her haunches, staring down at the building-place, but she could hardly focus enough to take in the longpaws' movements anymore. Her heart felt heavy in her rib cage.

How did that happen? How could I let myself do that?

She could not shake the image of Thorn's terrified eyes; they were burned into her vision. And she was haunted by the memory of such a tough, stubborn, stupidly courageous dog, lying trembling and submissive at her paws. *And all I had to do was growl at her.*

I would never have bitten her. Surely she knew that? Yes, I was angry and I lost my temper and I barked, but I wasn't going to bite!

But would the Pack ever believe that?

The thought hit her like that cage had done, slamming down onto her back. It was a horrible weight of misery and frustration and despair. *It doesn't matter what I do, and it doesn't matter how often I help the Pack or save any dogs. They are always watching me from the corner of their eyes, just the way Thorn did just now.*

They think there's a vicious monster inside me, just waiting to break out. They think it's only a matter of time.

And they will never, ever trust me....

CHAPTER NINETEEN

It was even more of a relief than usual when Storm's time at High Watch came to an end for the day. She trudged ahead of her companion down the cliff path, and Thorn made no attempt to catch up. The black-and-white dog had an air of utter dejection, and not a word had passed between her and Storm since their argument.

Something prey-sized rustled in the dry grass to Storm's flank, but she had neither the energy nor the enthusiasm to lunge for it. Instead, she plodded on down the cliff, thinking hard. *At least I have some peace to gnaw over things in my head. And at least I finally put an end to Thorn's stupid ranting. I guess there are some advantages to being a scary Fierce Dog.*

One by one, and only to herself, Storm counted off her list of suspects. She'd been thinking some more about the dogs who had already left the Pack. Chase had managed to visit her old friends quite easily in a single no-sun; she hadn't had to travel all that far. And that meant that, in turn, Rake, Ruff, Woody, and Dart were close enough to sabotage the camp and attack their former Pack-mates, if they wanted to.

Woody is quite a big dog, she remembered, *and he was always wild. He's a survivor, and pretty ferocious. Could he have sneaked back here and killed Bruno?*

I can't think of any reason Woody would have to attack the Pack, but then I never knew him very well. And I have to bear in mind—the fox said that it was a small dog who killed Bruno.

But that's so hard to believe! And even if that fox had a reasonable idea of the different sizes of dogs, can I trust what she says? Every dog knows foxes can't be trusted, and they've certainly harmed our Pack before.

One thing was for sure: Storm had reached the limit of what she could work out by herself. She would never solve the mystery if she didn't actively look for more information, more clues. *I need to talk to the dogs who knew the other dogs, the ones who left. That's the only way I'll ever get anywhere.*

By the time she reached the camp, a morose Thorn still trailing a rabbit-chase behind her, Storm knew what she had to do. *I could talk to Chase*—she shivered at the thought of trying—*but I doubt very much Chase would want to talk to me. It's not as if she'd give me any useful*

information about the defectors. She's their friend. No; I can't find out more
about the dogs who left the Pack without asking Breeze.

Luckily Breeze was easy to find; she was sprawled in the middle
of the glade, soaking up the late-afternoon rays of the Sun-Dog.
Storm padded over to her, grateful to be able to slump down on
the grass and relax. Breeze raised her head and gave a small *woof*
of greeting. For a moment Storm basked happily in the warmth,
rolling onto her back and forgetting her troubles; but it couldn't be
more than a moment. Sighing, she rolled back onto her belly and
touched her nose to Breeze's neck.

"Breeze, can I ask you a question?"

Breeze looked amused as she opened one eye and gazed fondly
at Storm. "You have a lot of questions, Storm. But of course I don't
mind. Go ahead!"

"This is going to sound like I can't let go of a bone, but . . ."
Storm hesitated, licking her jaws. "What did Woody think of
being in this Pack?"

Breeze pricked up her ears in surprise. "Woody?"

"Yes. I mean, there were many dogs who seemed to just go
along with the two Packs merging. It wasn't their actual *decision*,
but I guess they just accepted it at the time. I never really heard
Woody's opinion."

"Well." Breeze tilted her head, thinking. "He was fine with it to begin with, obviously. I don't think any dog would have joined the united Pack if they *hadn't* been. But then, he wasn't all right with it by the end. If he had been, he wouldn't have left, would he?" Breeze raised her brows at Storm, rather as if she thought the answer was too obvious for words.

Storm felt rather silly now, but she knew she had to press on. "Did he—did Woody get along all right with Whisper?"

Breeze looked even more astonished, if that was possible. "Why do you want to know that?"

Storm sighed, and closed her eyes briefly. "I don't know, it just seems to me that the bad dog doesn't *have* to be one who's still in the Pack. It might be one of the dogs who left. What do you think, Breeze? The night of Bruno's death, rain was pouring down. An outsider could easily have slipped into the camp and back out, and even if they'd left a trace, it would have been washed away in no time. Don't you think so?"

Breeze's lower jaw fell. "Why in the name of the Earth-Dog are you asking me, Storm?" Her voice was rising with her obvious shock. "How would I know how a dog would get in and out of camp unnoticed? I wouldn't have the first clue!"

Storm winced. She rather wished she hadn't asked. No wonder

Breeze sounded offended—she'd obviously had no clue why Storm would quiz her about Woody in the first place, and then to ask her how a dog might sneak in and out? *I should have stopped talking, about two questions ago. . . .*

But she did wish that Breeze would keep her voice down. Other dogs were turning their heads now, swiveling their ears toward Storm and Breeze. "Breeze, can you talk more quietly?" said Storm.

"Oh! I'm sorry." Breeze looked embarrassed. She dropped her voice. "Sorry, Storm. Look, I know you're finding it really hard at the moment. You seem to be on the wrong end of a lot of suspicion from the others, and that must be horrible for you. I know you want to find out who's responsible for all these awful things, but . . . but, Storm, can't you leave it alone for a bit?"

"I just can't do that," growled Storm in frustration. "It's so difficult, being with the Pack all day, and always watching, always wondering . . . never knowing which of these dogs is a traitor. I can hardly sleep at night."

Breeze was very quiet for a moment, gazing intently at a patch of grass. She scraped her claw across it, then raised her head and looked Storm full in the eyes.

"Storm," she said quietly, "maybe that's the answer. Maybe

being with the Pack, day in and day out, is just too hard for you."

"What?" Storm blinked.

"You can't let it go," Breeze went on, her voice urgent and sympathetic. "You're not getting a moment's peace while you're surrounded by the Pack, while any dog might be the culprit. And in the meantime, every dog seems to suspect *you*."

Storm licked her chops. "What are you saying?"

"I'm saying, maybe you should give things a chance to calm down. Give yourself a chance, too." Breeze's soft voice lowered still further. "You need to take a break from all this viciousness. Perhaps it's best if you leave the Pack for a while."

Storm started, her ears shooting up. Her heart beat hard in shock—yet somewhere deep down in her gut, she realized this was not a new idea to her. *Maybe I've been thinking this. Maybe I've been considering it for a long time, and I just didn't know.*

Maybe I've been denying it to myself. . . .

"Storm, *listen to me*." Gently Breeze touched Storm's nose with her own. "Let things die down. *Prove* it isn't you. If you're not here and—and Sky-Dogs forbid, something else happens—it will prove beyond doubt that you're not the guilty dog. Then they won't just welcome you back—they'll *beg* for you to come back. . . . They'll look to you to protect them. You'll be a hero to the whole Pack, Storm."

"I don't know, I . . ." The image Breeze presented had its attractions, she had to admit. *They'd beg for me to come back and protect them, would they . . . ?*

"I think you need to do this, Storm." Breeze nuzzled her unhappily. "I'd miss you so much—more than you know—but I honestly think it's the only way. And I'm saying this out of friendship. I don't *want* you to go, but I think you *have* to."

"I would miss the Pack." Storm's voice was huskier than she'd expected; she realized she could hardly get the words out. "I'll be lonely without all of you." And with those words, she realized with shock that she'd already moved on from *I would* to *I will*.

"I think every dog will miss you too," said Breeze, with a sudden anger in her eyes. "I think they will realize very quickly just how much they depend on you. How much you do, every day, for this Pack."

"Thank you, Breeze," croaked Storm. "That means a lot."

"And let's face it," Breeze said, nudging her gently. "When the supply of rabbits dries up, they'll soon understand what they're missing." She raised her voice again, quite deliberately. "You're the best hunter in the Pack, Storm, and every dog knows it."

Storm felt another twinge of embarrassment—*will Breeze never learn to talk quietly?*—but at the same time, she couldn't help feeling grateful and a little pleased. *She wants every dog to know what she thinks—that I'm a worthy member of this Pack. And I've no doubt she wants them to feel bad if I'm not around. . . .*

When *I'm not around . . .*

It felt good to have some dog on her side, even though it was almost too late. Storm had forgotten again how good that felt. And even if Breeze was only trying to cheer her up, she'd known exactly how to do it.

The smaller brown dog leaped suddenly to her paws, letting her tongue loll and bowing her shoulders in an invitation to play. "Come on, then, Storm. Catch me if you can!"

With a yip of delight, Storm sprang after her. Breeze dodged and rolled, nipping Storm's tail playfully. Storm doubled back and pounced, but let Breeze wriggle free again and dash in a circle.

It's only for a moment, but this is fun. Storm felt her worries slip away as she played and romped with Breeze in the glade. They were still waiting for her, all her horrible fears and anxieties—she could almost see them, like dark shadows waiting at the edge of the camp—but just for a little while, she could ignore them. Barking with excitement, Storm leaped for Breeze, and the two dogs tumbled over and over, wriggling and yapping and play-biting. Once more, Storm drew back to let Breeze slither out from between her forepaws and race away in a teasing circle.

I can't remember the last time I just played . . .

Breeze was pausing, wagging her tail in a taunting, tempting gesture, her head tilted as she grinned. Storm gave a mischievous bark and sprang for her.

Her forepaws thumped onto Breeze's back, and again the two of them crashed down in a heap. The brown dog was helpless beneath her paws—hah! Standing over her, Storm took Breeze's ear softly in her mouth and worried it. Her paws slipped on the grass and she planted one firmly on Breeze's leg for balance.

It was only when Snap barked, "Stop, Storm!" that she became aware something had changed. Blinking, she let go of Breeze's ear. Breeze's yelps weren't playful anymore. . . .

She was barking in pain.

Storm leaped away from her, horrified, and Breeze scrambled awkwardly to her paws. Storm took a cautious pace forward and nuzzled her friend.

"Are you all right?"

"I'm fine, I'm fine!" Breeze was breathless and her voice was a little shaky. She glanced around, looking embarrassed, at the Pack members who had rushed over when they heard her yelps. "I'm all right, for Earth-Dog's sake. Storm was only playing."

"What happened?" asked Mickey anxiously.

"Absolutely *nothing*," said Breeze firmly. "It was a game, and Storm landed a bit hard on my paw, that's all. There's nothing to worry about." She took a step toward Storm, as if in solidarity, but winced as she put down her paw.

"Breeze, you *are* hurt! I'm sorry." Storm licked her nose remorsefully.

"Oh, Sky-Dogs, don't worry! There's no need to apologize." Breeze sat down close to her. "It's my own fault. You're a big dog, and you don't know your own strength."

The Pack began to disperse, muttering and growling among themselves. Snap and Chase shot disapproving looks at Storm; Mickey shook his head a little sadly. Trying to ignore them, Storm lay down, head on her paws, and watched Breeze as she began to lick carefully at her hurt paw.

It was an accident. Breeze knows that, and she doesn't blame me.

But the Pack . . . I know how they'll see it. How they saw it. They've already made up their minds what happened: The Fierce Dog lost control. Again.

Storm gave a huge, miserable sigh.

And if I can hurt Breeze without even trying, without even knowing I was hurting her . . .

Maybe they're right.

* * *

She was running, running hard. It had never been more important to race as if Lightning himself were chasing her. Her paws pounded, her heart thrashed, her chest ached with the effort. But she had to run faster, and faster, bolting through the utter darkness.

She had to reach her quarry in time! He was ahead, just barely ahead. . . .

The Fear-Dog. The shadowy, menacing Spirit Dog flew before her, huge and terrifying. But why was he running away from her? Why should he flee? Why didn't he just turn, and snarl, and gulp her down his ravenous throat?

And suddenly Storm knew.

She knew why she was chasing the Fear-Dog. Gripped in those dark jaws, whimpering and mewling, was a golden pup.

It was Tumble—small, helpless, and vulnerable. And the Fear-Dog was carrying him away.

Straining every muscle and sinew, Storm sprinted after the horrific shadow. His giant haunches were always at the limit of her vision, dashing between the trees, and however fast she ran, she could not catch up. The Fear-Dog was silent, but she could hear Tumble's desperate, terrified cries. The Fear-Dog halted, turning to stare mockingly at Storm; Lucky and Alpha's pup dangled from his jaws.

"Help me, Storm," Tumble yelped. "Save me!"

Still she could not reach him. The Fear-Dog turned his rump on her once more, contemptuous, and bounded on.

Storm's breath burned in her throat and chest. She flew through the trees and burst out suddenly onto the beach that fringed the Endless Lake. Ahead of her the Fear-Dog raced; its massive paws left no marks in the sand, while Storm's sank and slithered on the shifting ground. The Fear-Dog and its terrified captive were drawing farther away! They were heading straight for the thundering white waves. Storm gave a desperate, wailing howl with her remaining breath.

The Fear-Dog was going to drown Tumble!

Storm's eyes snapped open and she gasped in a lungful of air. But with the air came cold, salty water, and she coughed and staggered to her paws. She sneezed, blinking in shock, and looked down. Her paws were submerged in the foaming waves of the Endless Lake.

No!

Snorting again, shaking her head and then her entire body, Storm snuffed at the bitter, salty air. She bounded onto dry sand. There was a scent she was half expecting, though she had thought it was only a dream. She sniffed again, to be sure, and her heart turned over in her chest.

Tumble. Tumble has been here!

She spun on her paws, tail stiff, her nostrils flaring wide and her eyes searching all around. There was no sign of the pup in the dim predawn light, though she was certain now that she had smelled him. *Yes, Tumble was here. But he isn't anymore. . . .*

Terrified, she turned again, staring out at the crashing waves of the lake. It could have swallowed him without a trace. *I would never know!*

Her eyes ached from scanning the bright surface in search of Tumble's golden coat, but she could see nothing. *Not that that means anything. The Endless Lake could eat a pup whole and barely even notice.*

Has Tumble gone in there? Has he drowned?

With a howl of frantic terror, Storm spun and raced back up the beach, heading for the Pack, terrible thoughts tussling in her mind. She'd dreamed about the pups in danger from the Fear-Dog before—but then she'd gone to the longpaw place, and there had been no scent of them, they had all been safe with the Pack. . . .

Whisper warned me that there would be a death in my dreams, and that came true.

What if she'd ignored her Fear-Dog dreams, but they were warnings too? What if something terrible had happened, because of her?

Where is Tumble?

CHAPTER TWENTY

Storm barely paused for breath as she leaped the thorny scrub at the edge of the camp, not bothering to find the easier entrance. Barks and howls rang in her ears; the Pack was already awake, and they knew something was wrong. Their voices collided, rising and falling, echoing into the forest till Storm couldn't tell which dog was barking.

"*Where's Tumble?*"

"*TUMBLE! Tumble, where are you?*"

"*Has any dog seen Storm? She's missing, too!*"

Lucky's panicked voice rose above the uproar. "Tumble! Tumble, my pup, answer me! Please!" He buried his nose in a tussock of grass, then abandoned it to race across to an old stump. "*Tumble!*"

As Storm burst out of the trees, every dog spun around, startled, and the volley of barks that met her felt like an incoming wave of the lake. Mickey and Snap dashed toward her, Chase in hot pursuit.

"Storm, where have you been?" yelped Mickey.

"What have you been doing?" barked Snap. "Tumble is missing!"

Daisy bolted between the two bigger dogs, her eyes pleading. "Storm, do you know where Tumble is? Have you seen him?" Behind her, Sunshine was yelping, too, but her cries were too full of distress to make any sense. Breeze, too, was howling incomprehensibly.

Alpha, though, was not howling or whining. She was silent, her face drawn with worry, but she stalked through the throng of dogs toward Storm with her teeth bared.

She was right in Storm's face when she stopped and barked, *"Where have you been? Where is my pup?"* Her dark eyes blazed. "You must have something to do with this, Storm! Where is Tumble?"

Storm felt a wrench of hurt, deep inside her chest. She opened her jaws to deny all knowledge, but the words would not come.

Maybe she's right. I did dream of Tumble. And I sleepwalked. I was at the Endless Lake.

And Tumble. He was there too, though I didn't see him.

Storm's heart turned over. *Did something happen to him while I was sleepwalking? Or . . . could the Fear-Dog really have taken him?*

"I was . . ." Her voice caught, as if there were a thorn in her throat. Every dog fell abruptly silent and stared at her.

"Yes, Storm . . . ?" Alpha's prompt held a growl of warning. "Speak!"

"I was at the lake." The admission rushed out of her, hot and shameful. "I went down there, because I . . . I couldn't sleep, and I . . ."

"You were at the lake?" Alpha's voice was cold and dangerous. She looked as if she was holding back terrible fear and anger, and there was no room for any other emotion right now. "And Tumble? Was he there, too?"

"He was—yes," croaked Storm.

A gasp went up from the Pack members, along with growls and exclamations of disbelief.

"Tumble had *been* there," she corrected herself, glancing from face to face. None of her Packmates looked sympathetic; they seemed only angry, and anxious, and confused. "I could smell him, I . . . but I couldn't *see* him. I couldn't see him anywhere. I did look, Alpha—I knew something was wrong, but he was nowhere in sight! And that's why I ran back just now—to tell you all . . ."

Her voice faltered. *I sound as if I'm lying. I sound like a dog with something to hide.*

And I am. But how can I tell them about my sleepwalking?

Every dog stared at her, their eyes narrowed. Snap exchanged a glance with Mickey. Sunshine looked miserable and a little suspicious. Twitch looked disappointed. Chase's eyes were downright hostile.

As for Alpha, Storm still didn't dare even look at her.

Chase snapped, "What were you doing there? At the lake?"

Storm turned toward the little dog, lowering her shoulders, pleading. "That doesn't matter right now. We have to get back to the lake and find Tumble!"

"Oh, but it *is* important," cut in Moon. She was standing farther back, looking thoughtful, but her eyes were hard. "You're often where you're not supposed to be. Where do you go, Storm? You're always sneaking around, turning up in odd places at odd times. What are we supposed to think?"

Dogs were nodding, murmuring agreement.

"It's true," muttered Snap to Mickey, loud enough for Storm to hear. "Even you can't deny that."

To Storm's horror, Mickey didn't. He said nothing, but he

didn't contradict his mate. And he wouldn't meet Storm's eyes.

"Wait a minute." The voice was Daisy's. The little white dog padded to Moon's side and stared up at her. "Storm's done nothing wrong," she barked.

"You don't know that—" began Moon, but Daisy shook her head.

"I do." Daisy turned to look at the rest of the Pack. "I know something the rest of you don't." She then turned her gaze on Storm, her black eyes apologetic. "Storm walks in her sleep."

"*What?*" barked Alpha.

Storm's rib cage felt heavy with dread and shame. *Oh, Daisy.* The little dog was trying to help her, she knew—but she wasn't sure this would make things better. *My secret. It's out. And I have a feeling it is only going to make things worse.*

"I've known for a while," Daisy admitted, padding up to Alpha and crouching in apology. "It's completely harmless. Storm didn't want you to know, so I kept quiet, but she doesn't do anything sinister."

"What *does* she do?" barked Chase. Other dogs yelped in echo of her question.

"She just walks." Daisy nodded at Storm. "That's all. She wanders around and she wakes up in odd places. There's nothing bad about sleepwalking. She can't help it."

For an instant, there was shocked silence. Then the Pack erupted in a cacophony of barking.

"This makes her *more* dangerous!" yelped Snap.

"Daisy, how could you keep this from us?" howled Chase. "You're the one who said we had to be honest with each other!"

"Storm walks around in her sleep and doesn't know what she's doing?" barked Moon in disbelief. "How can that possibly be innocent?"

"It may not be her fault," muttered Mickey, with a sideways apologetic look at Storm, "but it certainly does raise some questions."

"She could have been doing all the terrible things that have happened around here," yapped Chase, "and she wouldn't even know she was doing it!"

"No," whined Storm, trying desperately to make herself heard. "No, that's not possible. I couldn't have—"

"*Quiet!*" Alpha's sharp bark silenced every dog. She glared around at the Pack, finally letting her eyes come to rest on Storm. "This is something we can—*and will*—discuss later. For now, we have something much more important to do. Storm! You say you smelled Tumble, down at the Endless Lake?"

Storm nodded, relieved that, at least for now, she had a respite from their questions and accusations. "Yes, Alpha. His scent was there, and it was fresh. I'm sure of it."

"But he was nowhere in sight?"

"No! Or I'd have gotten him, no matter what, and brought him back to you!" Storm's eyes pleaded with her leader. *You have to believe me, Alpha.*

"Very well." Alpha nodded to Lucky, who looked somber and fearful. "Every dog to the beach, now—except for Sunshine. She will stay and watch the rest of the pups."

Sunshine nodded and scurried over to guard the three remaining pups. At once, with a summoning bark, Alpha leaped and bolted away into the forest, as fleet as the wind. Lucky was hard on her heels. The rest of the Pack fell in behind them, and Storm joined them, pounding through the trees as fast as she had in her terrible dream. *Faster.* A rising panic threatened to make her trip and stumble. *I don't understand any of this. How could I have dreamed such a vivid dream of Tumble, the very night he went missing?*

Her breath ached in her chest, just as it had in her dream. Her muscles stung with the effort. *It's as if I've run this route before.* She felt sick.

And just as she hadn't been able to catch the Fear-Dog, there was no way Storm could keep up with Alpha. She had never seen the swift-dog run so fast. Only when she reached the beach did Alpha finally slow to a halt, casting around with her raised muzzle for any trace of her pup.

"Spread out," she called, as one by one her Pack emerged panting from the trees behind her. "Look for any trace of Tumble. If Storm is correct, and he's been here, we should be able to find his trail easily enough."

Daisy, though last to arrive on her short legs, gave an immediate yelp. Every dog turned to her; she stood, tail quivering, beneath a small dune just next to the trees. "I have his scent over here!"

The dogs raced over, plunging through the soft, dry sand. Storm snuffled with the others, trying to follow Tumble's scent— but it petered out after only a rabbit-chase.

"That doesn't make sense." Mickey stood stiffly, his nostrils snuffling at the breeze. "How can his scent just vanish?"

"I've found it again!" barked Breeze. She was some way down the beach; sure enough, when the others ran to her side, they could smell the pup's distinctive scent once more. But yet again, it disappeared within a few paces.

It's as if he was carried, and set down now and again, thought Storm. *Carried in a big dog's jaws . . .* A thrill of horror went through her bones.

The Fear-Dog in my dream carried him like that!

"Here!" called Snap, who was farther down the beach, near the wet sand where the lake-tide reached.

This time only Mickey and Lucky ran to investigate; the other Pack members continued sniffing for Tumble in a wide arc across the sand. An occasional yelp signaled that a dog had picked up the scent again, but no dog managed to follow it for long. Alpha was lashing her tail in frustration, gazing around the beach in increasing desperation. Storm saw that her eyes were more and more frequently drawn to the crashing waves of the lake itself, and then they would fill with terror.

If Tumble's gone, Storm thought, *I can't imagine Alpha's and Lucky's grief. . . .*

Hesitantly Storm padded toward the water. It was hard to pick up any kind of scent on the sodden sand, beyond the smells of water grasses and crabs and salt, but she felt she had to try. *But if Tumble did go into the Endless Lake, what can I do? There will be nothing any dog can do.*

A memory came to her: Spring's limp body, floating in the lake after that terrible storm, one ear flopped over her dead eye. *Even the River-Dog couldn't have brought Spring back. If Tumble went into the water, there's no hope for him. . . .*

Wrapped in horrible thoughts, she barely heard the howling at first. Then it penetrated her thoughts: a piercing, summoning cry. "My Pack! My Pack!"

Alpha!

Storm's heart turned over in her rib cage, and she raced up the beach toward the sound. Other dogs were running too, from their searches across the wide bay, and they exchanged glances of fear as they converged on their leader.

The howl was coming from the bottom of the cliff, where two great slabs of gray stone had split and collapsed against each other. In the tiny gap between them, hidden by yellow grasses and scrubby brush, was a dark, cool cave. The echo of howling came from inside; Storm wriggled through into murky half-light, her Packmates behind her.

There stood Alpha, still howling her summons—in between frantic, furious licks to a cowering Tumble.

Storm felt dizzy; her heart raced and pounded with relief. The little pup's golden coat was sodden and dark, and he was trembling—but he was alive, and he seemed unharmed.

Lucky shoved past Storm to his mate's side, and he too fell to licking warmth back into his pup, his tongue almost knocking the little dog onto his side. "Tumble. *Tumble.* You're all right."

"We'll get you home," Alpha was murmuring as she licked the top of Tumble's golden head. She had stopped howling; the whole Pack was crammed into the cave. "We'll take you back to your sisters. We missed you so much, Tumble. Thank the Sky-Dogs we found you." She closed her eyes briefly, tilting her face toward the unseen sky.

"What happened to you, pup?" Mickey asked, his brown eyes huge.

Tumble opened his little jaws, but he was still shaking too much to speak. It took a lot more licking and nuzzling from his parent-dogs before he calmed down; the whole Pack waited patiently, tails wagging with relief and happiness.

"What happened, little one?" Alpha repeated at last, gently. "Why did you come here?"

He still quivered, and his voice shook. "I had to hide, Sweet. I had to hide!" He sounded small and terrified in the echoing darkness of the cave.

"Why, pup?" coaxed Lucky, licking his ears gently. "Why did you have to hide?"

"I don't know," he whimpered. "I don't know. She told me I had to hide."

Alpha and Lucky, startled, stared at each other over the pup's head. Then Alpha nuzzled him again. "Who, Tumble? Who told you to hide?"

In the silence, the little golden pup raised his trembling head. His whimper was barely audible.

"Storm did," he whispered. "Storm told me I had to hide."

"*What?*" Lucky's head snapped up, and he glared at Storm. Alpha lifted hers more slowly; again she gave Storm that cold, furious look.

Storm stammered, "Tumble, I—what—I don't unders—"

She took a pace toward him; he flinched back between his Father-Dog's paws, recoiling, pressing himself close to the ground.

Lucky looked down at him. Very softly, he asked, "Did Storm bring you here, pup?"

Tumble swallowed and nodded, quickly and frantically. "Yes," he whispered. "Storm picked me up and brought me. Storm was scary, Lucky!"

For a moment, Storm thought she was going to faint. There was no light of cunning in Tumble's eyes, no hint that he was lying or playing some strange pup-joke. He was scared, and shaking; and he was telling the truth. Storm's head whirled even as her heart plummeted in her chest.

"Lucky, I didn't. You have to believe me," she pleaded. "I can't have—I didn't—"

It's hopeless. And it isn't true. I obviously did.

But I never meant to do it.

"Lucky!" she blurted again. "I must have done it in my sleep. I—I didn't know! I didn't mean to. I would never hurt Tumble, you know that!"

Lucky didn't answer. If anything, he drew his protective paws closer around his trembling pup. Glancing up at her Packmates, Storm saw that, one by one, they were stepping back from her, drawing away. Their eyes were bright with fear and anger and mistrust. Even Daisy's . . .

Alpha spoke at last. "Pack," she said, and her voice was chillier than the water of the Endless Lake. "We must get Tumble back to the camp, and to his den. We cannot stay here. . . ." She glanced at Storm, then deliberately averted her eyes.

"We will talk about this later, as a Pack. The matter demands a proper gathering, and a Howl. But first, we must look after Tumble. The most important thing right now is that he's safe."

Lifting him gently in her jaws, Alpha carried her pup out of the cave and into the warm light of the Sun-Dog. Lucky followed her, and the rest of the Pack went behind him; not one of them looked back at Storm. She stood in the cold darkness of the cave and watched them all turn away.

The worst thing of all was that Storm couldn't blame them. They had every right to turn their rumps on her. Even Mickey and Daisy. *Especially* Lucky.

Oh, Sky-Dogs. The full horror of it rushed through her blood, swamping her, threatening to crush her.

What have I done?

CHAPTER TWENTY-ONE

Storm lay on her belly in the center of the camp. Her paws were in front of her and her head was raised; she didn't want to lower it to rest. Every member of her Pack sat in a circle around her, and despite her shame at what she had done, she did not want to look humiliated and beaten.

What I did was terrible. But I didn't mean *to do it.*

The late afternoon Sun-Dog breathed warmth on her back, but her blood felt cold. *I'll never be truly warm again.*

She blinked, gazing into the eyes of her Packmates. They were all quiet—some sullen, some hostile, some just miserable—as they waited for Alpha and Beta to emerge from their den. The two of them had vanished in there to settle Tumble back with his litter-sisters, but every dog knew they had also gone to discuss the way forward for the Pack. Twitch, the Third Dog, had been summoned inside after a while, and he had not yet reappeared.

Now the Pack awaited their leader dogs' decision in an unnatural, heavy silence.

Storm twitched an ear. She thought that even the birds must have caught the mood in the glade, for there was no singing. Somewhere, distantly, there was a crack of undergrowth as a group of deer moved through the forest, but no Pack Dog was thinking of prey right now.

Storm watched each dog's face, studying their expressions one by one. Not one of them would meet her eyes. *That's not good. . . .*

She could smell the mistrust on the air: the sharpness of suspicion and hostility. Some looked sadder than others—Mickey, Daisy, Sunshine, and Breeze—but still, they didn't dare look straight at her. Thorn and Beetle stared gloomily at the ground. As for Moon and Snap and Chase, their dislike was almost tangible.

They're all just waiting for Alpha's judgment, Storm thought. *They're waiting for her word before they tell me what they think. . . .*

But Storm realized, with a sudden clarity, that *she* didn't have to.

What am I waiting for? I know what I have to do.

I've known for a while now. It's something I should have done long ago.

The shadows crept across the glade, growing longer as the

Sun-Dog yawned and stretched and settled to his rest. Stars began to wink in the darkening sky. Beetles scurried in the grass and a lizard darted beneath a stone; Storm could hear the tiny creatures very clearly, as if all her senses were suddenly much sharper than they had ever been.

Maybe that's because I'm going to need them. Now more than ever.

At last there was movement at the entrance to Alpha's den; there was an audible sigh of relief throughout the Pack. Every dog seemed to tense in expectation, fur prickling and tails trembling.

Storm did not feel the general ripple of apprehension. She felt calmer than she had in a very long time as Alpha, Lucky, and Twitch emerged from the mouth of the den.

Their faces were very serious as they paced into the center of the glade. Storm rose to her paws and faced them squarely. Before Alpha could even open her jaws to speak, Storm took a single step forward.

"You don't need to say anything." Storm was glad that her voice sounded so level. "I know what you've talked about; well, it wasn't necessary."

Lucky sat back on his haunches, watching her nervously, but Alpha remained standing, listening intently as Storm spoke.

"*None* of you trust me now. Some of you never did, and

others . . . you trusted me when I helped find the pups, before, but ever since . . ." She cleared her throat and licked her jaws. Perhaps she shouldn't have mentioned the pups—Alpha's expression turned hard, and several of the others were staring at her as if they couldn't believe they had felt so kindly toward her. "And after what happened with Tumble, I can't blame you. I don't deserve your trust."

Some of the dogs shuffled uncomfortably and shared awkward glances; others gaped at her, but all remained silent.

"There's something I want to say, Alpha." Storm looked levelly at her leader. "With my waking mind and body, I would never, ever do anything to harm this Pack. I'm sorry I kept my sleepwalking a secret; that was a mistake, and I'm sorry. I know I don't have it in me to harm any of you—least of all the pups. But *you* don't know that. You have no way of knowing it, and I can't prove it. So I understand why all of this makes you so nervous."

Alpha gave a single, slow nod.

"I also want to say," Storm went on, her gaze roaming over each Pack member, "that I still think there's an enemy dog walking among you. And it isn't me, however bad this situation might look. Telling a pup to hide, putting him in danger without knowing I was doing it—that looks terrible. I'm sorry that I scared

Tumble; I never meant to cause him harm. But picking up a pup in your sleep is one thing. Murdering a Packmate is another thing altogether."

Alpha and Lucky shared a look, Storm noticed. They both looked unconvinced, and that hurt Storm like broken clear-stone in her belly.

She drew a heavy breath. "But even though I didn't mean to, I did put Tumble in danger. And that's why I can't stay in this Pack any longer." Storm raised her head, blinking hard. "I'm leaving. It's the only way."

She closed her eyes briefly in the silence that followed. Her calm was beginning to crumble now. *Hold it together, Storm, just a little longer. . . .*

She suppressed a shudder and gazed around the Pack. Mickey and Daisy still looked sad, Sunshine had lain down on her belly, her face resting miserably on her forepaws. Beetle and Thorn looked a little shocked. But no dog protested; no dog moved or barked out that she should stay. Storm felt as if her heart were twisting and wrenching inside her, as if it were being bitten by a hungry fox.

I know I have to leave. Everything I've said is true.

But it hurts that none of them want me to stay.

Alpha still said nothing, and neither did Lucky. The two leaders, with Twitch, stood and watched as Storm backed up a few paces. At last, taking a deep, ragged breath, she turned her rump on the Pack. One pace, then two, then a third: Storm strode determinedly out of the glade and across the camp boundary.

She could still hear no whines or barks behind her; the Pack was watching her leave in complete silence. She carried on placing one paw in front of the other. Storm realized she wasn't even aware what direction she was going; she simply kept padding on, putting a rabbit-chase between her and her former Packmates, then another, and another. With each step it became a little easier to keep walking, despite the terrible ache in her rib cage and belly.

I hate leaving. But I have to leave.

They don't trust me, and it hurts. But they have good reason.

Keep walking, Storm. Just keep going.

Images came into her head, making her gut twist with pain: Daisy's cheerful face, Mickey's wagging tail as he bounded ahead of her on a hunt. Moon's exasperated expression as she heard of more antics from Beetle and Thorn. Breeze, curled around the pups, protecting them as they slept; and Sunshine, waving her raggedy plume of a tail for Tiny to chase.

There are lots of dogs I will miss. Even the ones who didn't trust me. They were my Pack, and I may never see them again. . . .

Storm came to a halt and shook herself violently. She gave a ferocious growl, curling her muzzle.

Be strong, Storm! These thoughts aren't helping.

The Pack would be better off without her; she had to believe that, despite what Breeze had said about her being the best hunter. And she would certainly be better off without the Pack. It had become impossible: the wary glances, the muttered remarks. Life as a Lone Dog would be simpler, more relaxing; she wouldn't always have to watch her words, she wouldn't have to pad so carefully around the anxieties of her Packmates. If she wanted to snarl with rage and bite her own tail in frustration, she could do it without striking terror into every dog in earshot.

Lucky survived for a long time as a Lone Dog. He was happy, and he hunted alone. I can do the same. I can be happy too.

She had walked a long way already, it struck her as she came out of the trees onto a long, grassy slope. The Sun-Dog lit the landscape with his last, slanting rays; he was a bright point of dazzling gold on the far horizon. Every leaf and blade of grass glowed with the great Spirit Dog's light.

And then, abruptly, there was another, separate flash of gold.

It sprang up from nowhere and stood poised before her, bright and magnificent:

The Golden Deer!

Storm halted and stared, awestruck by its beauty. It was standing so close to her, she could see straight into its bright liquid-bronze eyes. The tines of its antlers sparkled with points of light and its hide shone like the Sun-Dog himself.

Storm's aching heart pounded, and her throat felt dry and tight. The beauty and solemnity of the creature was overwhelming, and for long moments she could only gape at it, dazzled.

It looked back at her, unafraid, challenging.

One leap. One good spring is all it would take. I could bring down the Golden Deer right here, right now; it's as if the Wind-Dogs have sent it to me.

If I take the Golden Deer, the Pack will have good fortune at last. The pups will be safe, and happy, and that will be down to me. Tumble, Fluff, Nibble, and Tiny: They'll thrive and be truly lucky.

If I catch the Golden Deer for my Pack . . .

For the Pack.

Storm and the Golden Deer just gazed into each other's eyes, as the last rays of the Sun-Dog faded. The glowing light died from the landscape, and shadows crept across the grass and the trees.

But still the Golden Deer remained radiant, as if a part of the Sun-Dog had stayed here with it.

It blinked at her, slowly. Storm dipped her head, once, in awed respect.

And then she turned away.

She padded across the dew-damp grass without looking back. She walked on, away from the Golden Deer, and felt no regret at all. She walked until she knew that even that beautiful, shining Spirit Deer had faded from view and disappeared in the shadows of the night.

It isn't my duty anymore. I'm a Lone Dog now. I can't bring good fortune to a Pack that is no longer mine.

DON'T MISS

THE GATHERING DARKNESS

SURVIVORS

BOOK 5:
THE EXILE'S JOURNEY

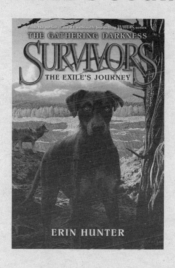

The world is a cold and hungry place for a Lone Dog, and Storm feels more lost than ever. There are only two dogs she knows will never give up on her—Arrow, her fellow Fierce Dog, and his mate, Bella. But to find them, Storm must fight through longpaw dangers, Leashed Dogs, and a forbidding Pack of wolves, all in search of a place where she might finally belong.

CHAPTER ONE

I've really messed this up.

Storm's paws skittered across the pale sand, kicking it up behind her as she ran, but she knew she'd never be able to run fast enough.

The big white cliff-bird gave a hoarse shriek, flapped its huge wings, and launched into the air.

It had been sunning itself on a jutting rock in the middle of the beach with its head tucked under its wing: the perfect prey, if Storm had only been patient enough to go around the rock, instead of trying to climb it.

But hunger had made her careless. She'd lost her footing and sent a cluster of pebbles scattering under her paws, and the bird had taken flight.

Instinct told Storm to leap after it, but her weak and tired muscles wouldn't obey her, and she slithered to an undignified stop, her front paws buried in the sand.

She snorted in annoyance at herself as she watched the bird fly off. A good meal, just flapping away into the sky. It was such a waste.

Storm scrabbled out of the sand and shook herself. She trudged on along the edge of the Endless Lake, trying to ignore the rumbling in her belly.

The Sun-Dog's light glinted off the water. It was still and calm today. The sky was clear and cloudless. Storm felt like her fur had only just dried out from the warm rain that had driven all the small prey into their holes and burrows last no-sun, but she could also feel a prickling in her nostrils that told her Lightning and Thunder might be close, and creeping closer on soft paws.

She had to keep going. Perhaps there would be another pool with those little darting brown fish—although they had been barely more than a mouthful for Storm. They were never going to fill her stomach, no matter how easy they were to catch.

Walking on the sand felt harder than it had before. It slipped out from underneath Storm's paws, and she kept losing her balance. She remembered Bella showing her how to keep her tread light so that she wouldn't sink, but she couldn't seem to muster the energy anymore. The skin on her flank and her belly hung loosely.

Would the Pack think I was a big, scary Fierce Dog now? she thought bitterly.

Hunting alone was harder than she'd expected. And, which was almost worse, it was no fun at all. She had only her own eyes to spot prey with, only one nose to scent it with. She didn't have a Scout Dog running ahead to root out the next prey creature. No dog would help her head off a rabbit if it startled, or talk through her tactics with her before she sprang, or reassure her that she would catch something soon when she failed.

She *knew* that Lone Dogs could survive without a Pack, but at the moment she was struggling to see how.

Storm flopped down on the warm sand and let the heavy salt stench of the Endless Lake fill her nostrils.

It smelled of home, but there was something missing. The scents of the Wild Pack.

Several journeys of the Sun-Dog had passed since she had left their camp behind and set out on her own. She had passed the farthest reach of the Patrol Dogs' scent a long time ago. She'd passed the Light House and shuddered as she remembered poor Spring, washed away when the Wild Pack and the Fierce Dogs had faced off on the narrow hardstone path that led to it.

She was farther from the Pack now than she had ever been before.

I should forget about them. Even if I did want to go back, they wouldn't have me.

In her mind's eye, she could still see them—Alpha and Beta with their pups, Mickey and Snap, Breeze, Chase, Moon and Beetle and Thorn, little Sunshine, and Daisy. . . .

Daisy, who Storm had thought was her friend. But then when it counted, even the small white dog had turned on her.

Storm shook her head and huffed, making tiny specks of sand dance in front of her muzzle. She knew that wasn't fair. She was just grumpy because she was hungry.

Still, it had hurt when Daisy had piped up, *I know something the rest of you don't. Storm walks in her sleep.*

Storm stared out at the Endless Lake, a shiver running through her body, despite the warmth of the Sun-Dog on her flanks. She was remembering. . . .

The Fear-Dog flew before her, huge and terrifying. Gripped in his dark jaws, whimpering and mewling, was a golden pup.

It was Tumble—small, helpless, and vulnerable. And the Fear-Dog was carrying him away.

The memory of the dream still seemed almost as vivid as it had that no-sun. She had been so convinced that the Fear-Dog itself was about to drown Tumble . . . but it had been *her* who had carried the pup to the Endless Lake and left him shivering in a cave, all alone, in the dark. She'd woken up on the beach and run back to the Wild Pack, frantic with worry, not remembering what had happened until Tumble was found and he explained it to his Mother-Dog in a trembling, squeaky voice.

Why did I do it?

Storm knew she might have done the wrong thing, hiding her sleepwalking from them. But she'd done it because she'd known that they would be afraid of her.

And, sure enough, they had been.

None of the Pack trusted her anymore, and how could Storm blame them? She couldn't trust herself. It was better that she'd left. It was better that she was . . . alone.

The Endless Lake gave a soft growl, as if it too was angry with her, and its white, wet paw rose out of the water and crashed on the beach nearby. Storm clambered awkwardly to her paws. The Lake-Dog was right—it wouldn't do any good to lie here and dwell on something she couldn't change.

There was a path close by that led up the cliffs and away from the Endless Lake, through scrubby grass where she thought she might find some small prey, or another chance to catch a cliff-bird. She had to keep trying.

Her paws felt shaky at first on the more solid ground, but soon she was clambering up over the rocks and between tall, spiky bushes with long stems that looked like fuzzy dogs' tails.

She sniffed the ground as she walked, and suddenly, as she reached a single, drooping tree, she smelled something familiar.

That's a dog!

Her ears pricked up, and she took a great sniff of air. A dog had definitely come this way—probably stopped beside this tree, perhaps even slept here. Was it one of the Wild Pack? She couldn't make out the particular scent. And what would they be doing this far from their camp? Maybe it was another dog altogether.

She sniffed harder, but the scent was starting to fade. She could tell now that it was stale. It had been at least a journey of the Sun-Dog since another dog had passed this way. Wishful thinking had made it seem fresher than it was. Storm walked on.

I'm alone. And that's fine.

The Sun-Dog continued on his journey, and still Storm couldn't find any prey she could catch. There had been a rabbit warren, but it was empty. She had given up on trying to catch squirrels before they ran up trees—her limbs felt weak and clumsy, and she couldn't leap or balance on her thin back legs.

She moved away from the Endless Lake, turning inland but always keeping the scent of the lake on her left, so she could be sure she was moving farther and farther from the Wild Pack. She walked through a thick wood of pine trees, the needles bursting with scent as she trod over them. Then she climbed up a rocky slope and found herself looking down the other side at the steep, muddy bank of a river.

It was much less full than the river that she knew—the one where she had finally beaten Blade on the ice, and where she and Lucky had taught the pups that they didn't need to be afraid of the River-Dog. This was like the smaller littermate of that river, a wide muddy basin with only a trickling stream winding between the rocks and a few sprouting green stalks.

Did the River-Dog not like this place? Was her attention turned elsewhere? Or was this the very end of the other river's tail? Did it run in a big loop around the Pack's territory?

Across the stream, Storm looked up and saw more pine trees, rising toward something strange in the distance. It took her a long moment of staring to realize that it was like a hill—but taller than

...ny she had ever seen before. It rose up and up and up into the sky, so big it vanished into the clouds and she couldn't even see the top.

Could a dog walk that far? Could they live in the sky, near the clouds?

Storm shook herself—she would never make it that far if she didn't find something to eat. Still, she couldn't help feeling a stir of adventure in her heart. A dog without a Pack could go wherever she wanted, couldn't she?

I wonder what Lucky would say if he saw this. . . .

For now, she decided to follow the stream. Perhaps she could catch something on the edge of the water. If she walked in the mud, the prey wouldn't catch her scent.

She had gone a few rabbit-chases when, sure enough, a bird landed on a rock sticking out in the middle of the stream. It was really big, even fatter than the cliff-bird, with black feathers that glistened as a few drops of rain began to fall.

More rain, Storm sighed. She would have found somewhere to shelter—but the bird was paying her no attention, searching in the mud of the river bottom, probably looking for worms.

Storm crept closer, ignoring the rain, keeping her head low to the ground, moving as slowly as she dared. She was glad she was downwind, even though birds didn't seem to scent things the way dogs did.

The drops of rain were growing heavier and closer together, splashing in the mud at her paws and beating across her back. She blinked water out of her eyes, focused only on her prey. The rain was good—it would muffle the sound of her approach, as well as her scent. The mud was growing stickier and slipperier, but she kept her footing, even though she knew she would have to spend a long time later getting the earth out from between her toes.

The bird was hunched now, its feathers ruffled up around its neck, as if it was making the same decision as Storm—*shelter, or food?* Storm was a few pawsteps from being close enough to pounce when its neck suddenly rose and its beak twisted around, sending raindrops spinning off into the air. But it wasn't looking at Storm—it was looking farther upstream, toward something Storm couldn't see. It took flight with another arcing spray of water and vanished into the trees.

"*Sky-Dogs!*" Storm growled. "Can't I have one piece of good—"

She broke off. Something was happening. The mud around her paws was washing away. The stream had grown wider and deeper, surrounding Storm and covering most of the muddy basin. Even as she stood still, the water buffeted at the ground underneath her, and she struggled to keep her balance. Then there was a wet crashing sound, and up ahead, a wall of water sloshed around the corner of a rock, right toward Storm.

River-Dog! Help me! Storm thought, trying to turn and scramble for the bank, but the stream underpaw was a river now, and she splashed and slipped as she turned. The wave hit her while she was off-balance, knocking her off her paws. She rolled over and spun around, trying to reach for something solid to hold on to, but there was nothing but mud and water. The river closed over her head. Freezing panic seized her throat, and she paddled as hard as she could against the River-Dog's current, breaking the surface just long enough to feel the air and rain on her muzzle before she was pushed under again.

This was worse than splashing in the Endless Lake, with its constant push and pull, and much worse than the steady river she knew—the River-Dog was running as if she was being chased by something!

Storm kicked out and broke through the surface again, just in time for another wave to crash over her, blinding her for a moment. There were no scents except for mud and panic.

You're a big, strong Fierce Dog, she thought. *It's just water!*

But the water was so big, and Storm felt very small, as if she was still a pup and she would be swept away if Martha didn't come to her rescue any moment.

In fact, through the splashing waves and the pounding rain, she thought could almost see the enormous water-dog, her giant black paws striking the surface as she swam with the current toward Storm.

She was so swift and graceful in the water. . . .

Storm couldn't breathe without sucking in water, and the cold was making her legs ache as she scrambled for a hold on the mud, but she thought she saw Martha moving toward her, and a small voice in her mind said, *It'll be all right, Martha will save us.* Her panic subsided.

But then the shape reached Storm and passed.

Martha, wait! Storm twisted to follow the dark dog-shape. Martha was leaving her behind! Storm tossed her head back and tried to copy Martha's swimming movements, just as she and Grunt and Wiggle had done as pups, just as she'd taught Lucky and Sweet's pups to do.

As she swam, the dark shape became less like a dog and more like a wave. It rolled and vanished into the water. Storm swam on, exhausted and grateful to Martha—or had it been the River-Dog?

Perhaps it was both. Between them, they had sent her a memory.

Sometimes, the worst thing you can do is fight the current, Martha had said. *A dog can never win that fight.*

And sure enough, it was easier to stay above the water now that she was facing the same direction as the wave and not trying to fight it. She could even push herself off small rocks and move, bit by bit, over toward the bank.

Finally, the mud beneath her was solid enough for her to dig in her claws, and she half-dragged herself and half-ran out of the water and up onto solid, sticky ground. She stumbled and crawled along the bank until she was away from the river, on ground that was thick with grass and thin, creaking saplings.

She flopped down, her flanks heaving.

Martha, thank you.

The breath rasped in Storm's throat and the rain beat down on her, but she didn't mind. It was washing some of the mud from her fur, and when she caught a little on her tongue, it tasted fresh and clean.

Just stop fighting. Turn and ride the current, she thought. *Oh, Martha. Perhaps if I'd listened to you, I would have left the Wild Pack long ago. . . .*

Fighting her Packmates' fears had been like trying to swim

upstream into a rushing tide. It was a fight that Storm was never going to win. The knowledge was uncomfortable, like lying here in the grass in the rain, but if she hadn't made that decision, their terror would have drowned her.

ERIN HUNTER

is inspired by a fascination with
the ferocity of the natural world.
As well as having great respect for
nature in all its forms, Erin enjoys
creating rich, mythical explanations
for animal behavior. She is also the
author of the bestselling Warriors,
Seekers, and Bravelands series.

Visit the Packs online at
www.survivordogs.com!

ENTER THE
BRAVELANDS

Heed the call of the wild in this action-packed series from **Erin Hunter**.

WARRIORS: THE PROPHECIES BEGIN

In the first series, sinister perils threaten the four warrior Clans. Into the midst of this turmoil comes Rusty, an ordinary housecat, who may just be the bravest of them all.

Also available as audiobooks!

WARRIORS: THE NEW PROPHECY

In the second series, follow the next generation of heroic cats as they set off on a quest to save the Clans from destruction.

WARRIORS: POWER OF THREE

In the third series, Firestar's grandchildren begin their training as warrior cats. Prophecy foretells that they will hold more power than any cats before them.

HARPER
An Imprint of HarperCollinsPublishers

www.warriorcats.com

WARRIORS: OMEN OF THE STARS

In the fourth series, find out which ThunderClan apprentice will complete the prophecy.

WARRIORS: DAWN OF THE CLANS

In this prequel series, discover how the warrior Clans came to be.

HARPER
An Imprint of HarperCollinsPublishers

READ EVERY SEEKERS BOOK

Seekers: The Original Series

Three young bears . . . one destiny.
Discover the fate that awaits them on their adventure.

Seekers: Return to the Wild

The stakes are higher than ever as the bears search for a way home.

Seekers: Manga

The bears come to life in manga!